the girl in the WELL is ME

the Girl in the WELL is ME

Karen Rivers

SCHOLASTIC INC.

ISBN 978-1-338-11144-6

12 11 10 9 8 7 6 5 4 3 2 1   16 17 18 19 20 21

Printed in the U.S.A.   40

First Scholastic printing, September 2016

Design by Carla Weise

for Lola—
JE t'aime.

1

Fallen

The whole thing feels like a prank at first, like something they planned—a joke with a punch line. Maybe, before I know it, one of the girls will tell me it's meant to be funny and then get me out of here.

But then again, maybe not.

I have a bad, bad, bad feeling about this.

I try not to panic. The first thing everyone says to do in emergencies—earthquakes or house fires or if, say, you fall down an abandoned well out in the wasteland behind town—is to stay calm.

"Stay calm, Kammie," I tell myself. My voice echoes up the dusty shaft to where the girls are, safe on high ground. I kind of think of them as The Girls, with capital letters like that. I think that's how they think of themselves.

"HELP!" I scream. "MANDY KANDY SANDY!"

I am thoroughly wedged, arms pinned against my sides. No one answers me, but I know they are up there.

I can hear my own breathing.

I'm panicking.

No! I'm not panicking. I won't.

My feet are dangling over nothing. I can feel all that emptiness underneath them, cold and bottomless.

I try to breathe slow, in and out. In and out. In and out. My heart beats. Nothing is broken, at least I don't think so. So I guess I'm OK.

I *am* OK.

I will be OK.

OK.

I'm not actually OK and it hurts to breathe. It

hurts to *be*. I scream "HELP!" again. But it hurts even more to scream, so I stop.

"Guys?" I call. "This isn't funny." Why aren't they answering? I know they are there. I hear gravel crunching under their feet and the sound of voices, low and too quiet to understand, whispers that float by in the sky above the well's now-open mouth.

"KANDY!" I scream. "HELP!" Kandy is in charge. Kandy is the one to ask. She is The Queen of them all.

I stare up at the perfectly round hole of sky and hot Texas air, and wait. And then—finally—there they are, three shadowy faces peering down at me from the top of the well, filling up all that blue. Mandy, Kandy, and Sandy, the most popular girls in the sixth grade at Nowheresville Middle School. Their mouths are open, like it might help them to see me better.

"Wow," Sandy says. "You fell in." I guess Sandy is in charge of stating obvious things.

"I fell in." I'm crying now. "I fell in!" I repeat. "This isn't funny. Get me out!"

The sun is angled so there is just one ribbon of light on the wall in front of me. There is not much else to look at except the blue hole up there, and craning my neck is starting to hurt. The wall is yellowish-brown dusty brick. Or maybe it's ancient clay. The dust makes me think of old people's skin, crumbling and dry.

"Help me please, help me please . . ." I whimper, pulling my face back as far from the wall as I can. I don't want to be breathing in old-person skin dust! I cough. Why aren't they getting me out of here?

"HELP ME NOW," I yell. "PLEASE?"

"WAIT," a voice answers. "Just . . . hang ON."

"And, like, stop shouting," another one says. I don't know them well enough to be able to tell without looking whose voice is whose. I look up.

A foot is dangling over the edge, like the owner of the foot is just sitting there casually. The foot is wearing blue nail polish. My mom would kill me before she'd let me wear that color on my nails, that's for sure. She's old-fashioned, she says. She doesn't think nail polish is "appropriate" for kids, even though she used to wear it all the time, back when she used to get pedicures. Probably the same color, even. I stick my tongue out at the foot, not that it can see me, and it vanishes back out of sight. The owner of the foot is probably thinking, *What if it gets dirty? Gross.*

I am covered with dirt. So I guess that *I* am gross. I sneeze three times, *bang bang bang*, and little clouds of dust float between me and the sun, hovering like filthy fairies.

This, as my grandma would say if she wasn't dead, is a fine kettle of fish. Luckily for me, there are no fish in the well—or water, thank goodness. I *hate* fish, with their puckered mouths that look like they are going to suck the flesh clean off your bones, tiny bit by tiny bit, like little sea vampires.

I may be 11 years old, but I'm very small for my age. If I wasn't so small, I wouldn't have been able to slip so easily into the bricks and mortar and whatever else holds well walls together when the old, dirt-covered board I was standing on gave way and let me drop into the hole like a whack-a-mole.

Except I can't pop back up. If I was a normal size, this wouldn't be happening. If this was a wishing well and I had a coin, I'd wish to be bigger. I'd wish to be huge. I'd wish to be the tallest girl in the sixth grade, the tallest girl in the world. I hate being small. It's just not fair.

The only time being small pays off is when you are trying to get a discount on movie tickets. And even then, it's not worth it because getting away with that is the same as lying. Lying turns your soul into something small and dry and hard, like an old raisin you find in your book bag squashed under a book you on-purpose-forgot to return to your old school library because you loved it too much to leave it behind.

I hereby declare that I, Kammie Summers, age 11, am not a liar, which is a *miracle*, if you consider where I come from. My parents are the biggest liars of all: If there was a prize for lying, they would win it by a mile. Their souls are worse than raisins, they are tiny lumps of coal, squashed so hard that maybe they're turning into diamonds, sharp and glittery.

My soul? Well, it's still *basically* a grape, sweet and juicy and delicious and, frankly, kind of awesome.

Which doesn't even *matter*, because my juicy and amazing soul is *stuck in a well*.

"KANDY!" I yell. "GET ME OUT! NOOOOOOOWWWWWW!"

Kandy Proctor's face appears above me. "Kammmmmmmmmmie," she drawls, sing-songy and slow, like *What's the rush?*

Kandy is also 11, but is not small for her age. Her head starts slowly moving lower and lower into the hole. Someone must be holding on to her legs to stop her from falling. Kandy Proctor is not the kind of girl who falls into wells. From this angle, her chin looks like it's made of Silly Putty, pulling stringily away from her neck. "Holy cow," she says. "You're far." She stretches her arm down the well, but can't even reach the tip of my nose, which is my highest point right now. Her fingernails are blue. And those blue nails, they aren't anywhere near close enough to touch me. Panic bubbles up in my throat. I swallow it like hot soup and it hurts and burns. She waves her arm around. "So, grab on, I guess!" she says. There is something about the way that Kandy moves that makes me think of a giraffe, long and bony.

She's too far away.

"I can't reach up!" I shout. I'm mad now. "My *arms* are stuck! How can I grab on? How am I going to get out?"

"Are you dying?" she asks, ignoring the question. "Like, are you . . . broken?"

"No!" I yell. "And no! I don't know! It hurts. I hurt. Why did you let me fall in the well?" Specifically what Kandy had said was, "Stand on that square right there." She'd pointed at a square of dirt that was slightly higher than the dirt around it, the thing that was covering the well. "And sing a song, loud, but not a Christmas song because I really hate those. Sing something good. And you have to get *all* the words right, or you have to start over."

I did it, just what she said. Or, at least, I tried to.

I had gotten as far as *the dawn's early light* when the wood under me snapped in two like someone had given it a kung fu punch, and down I went. I'd thought I was winning. I mean, I knew all the words and no one is going to say that the national anthem isn't cool. There's no way.

"Um," Kandy says now. "I kind of don't know why you didn't test the board before you stood on it?" Her hair, which is in a braid, swings like a rope. If this was a real working well, it would have a bucket tied to it. The bucket would land on my head. And she'd probably laugh.

"I hate you!" I whisper. Then louder I go, "I don't know. But you have to get me out!"

"Kammie," she says. "Stay calm, girl. OMG, the blood is totally rushing to my head. I feel sick. Are you going to grab me or not?"

I think she's a little bit in love with how caring she's trying to sound, but her OMGs and her concerned voice make me feel like I'm watching her audition for the school play. From the bottom of a well, that is. "I. Can't. Reach!" I yell. "OMG, Kandy," I mimic her. "Just get me out."

"I don't know how! Um," she says, "I'm seeing

stars. Like in a cartoon! Sorry. I'll be back in a sec."
Her hand and her braid and her face all disappear
in an upwards flush of swirling Kandy drama. I
hear a giggle and a thump.

I try to stop breathing so fast. I try to stop being
so mad at Kandy. And Mandy. And Sandy. (Which
is kind of impossible, but I *try*.) I also try to think
about what to do. But all I can think is *HELP! I'M
GOING TO DIE!* And also, *OMG OMG OMG*.

I guess Kandy is rubbing off on me after all.
Back in my old life, I'd never say "OMG." I wasn't
one of those girls. I was different. I used bigger
words. But now I'm here, and I'm just a small-
worder. I'm someone who says "LOL." Or, "I want
a BFF." I don't even know who I am anymore, to
tell you the truth. And it doesn't matter. Because
I'm in a well.

I try to pretend like I'm playing the part of a kid
in a public service announcement about dangerous
wells, except if I was, then the camera would stop
rolling and someone would get me out. And/or I'd
know how to get MYSELF out. Because someone

would tell me how! That's the great thing about acting: Someone always tells you how to be and what to do. I *love* acting. Drama is my favorite—or, at least, it was. There is no Drama Club here in Nowheresville, Texas. There are sports, sports, and more sports. And stupid cheerleading classes, so maybe—if you try real hard—you can be a cheerleader for all those sports in high school.

No thank you.

I'd rather do the sports, even though I hate sports.

But maybe if I was sportier, I could climb out of here. Maybe if I was more muscly, I wouldn't have fallen down here in the first place. Maybe if I was someone else, I wouldn't have been gullible enough to stand on a well in the first place.

"HURRY!" I yell. "Hurry, hurry, hurry!"

I can hear the rise and fall of the girls' voices, the scuffling of shoes in the gravel-crunchy dirt, the giggling. The pauses while they try to think of something. They could easily walk away. They could go and not come back. My stomach does a twist. I swallow hard, dust in my throat, trying not to be sick. Let's face it, there is nowhere for throw-up to go in here except to puddle on my chest, which would basically be the worst.

Like this could get worse.

The blue sky, which is no longer blocked by Kandy Proctor's head, or anyone else's for that matter, is as round as a coin up there. The sun, which has edged into view, is burning a shadow in my vision. "There is a light at the end of the tunnel," I yell. "But I can't reach it!" I'm trying to be funny. Gallows humor, Mom would call it. We have a lot of that around our house lately.

"Don't go to the light!" shouts Sandra Fishburn, suddenly appearing, blinking, above me. Sandy's dad is a preacher. She's kind of both too dumb and too serious for that joke to work. "Don't go to the light! If you go, you *won't* come back. People don't."

"I'm stuck," I say. "I can't *go* anywhere. And the light is the sun! Not, like, *the light of heaven*! I was kidding. But, come on, Sandy. Come on. What are you guys doing up there? Help me."

"Kammie," Amanda Fassbender says, her face now in the gap next to Sandy's. "This is getting boring. Just, just, just . . . get out of there!"

"I CAN'T GET OUT," I shout. "I CAN'T MOVE!" Kandy appears alongside the others and all three girls stare down at me. It's hard to tell what their faces are doing. "GET HELP!" I add, helpfully. "PLEASE!" I don't want to be crying, but I can't stop it. There's snot and tears all over my face, mixing with the dust. I must look disgusting. It's like my face is pouring tears out all over the place without my say-so. "I don't know what you're doing!" I hiccup. "Help me. I don't like it in here!"

"No one likes wells," Mandy says. "Except maybe snakes or lizards, and stuff like that."

"WHAT?" I yell. "WHAT?"

"Calm down. I was joking!" Mandy says. "Sort of. I mean, there probably aren't any snakes in there. . . ."

Kandy snort-laughs. "There aren't!" she says. "Don't let Mandy freak you out."

"I AM ALREADY FREAKED OUT," I yell.

I hope there aren't snakes down here. A well

actually does seem like a place where a snake would like to live. Do snakes like to be cold? I can't remember. Maybe I never knew. I don't know much about snakes. They are either warm-blooded or cold-blooded, which means they either like to be cold or hate it. I shiver and pull my arms and legs tighter into my body, and I slip down again. Farther.

Deeper.

No!

The little patch of light that was on the wall is gone now. There is nothing in front of me but shadows and darkness.

"STOP!" I yell at myself and somehow I do. I cross my feet at the ankles then uncross them. My feet wish they had something to stand on. My feet are desperate to stop my fall. I could fall forever. I could fall out the other side of the world.

"Don't go deeper!" yells Kandy, like it's a choice that I can make.

"Kandy," says Sandy, in a whisper so loud it echoes down into my ears and rubs up against them, Styrofoam-sinister. "What if we can't get her out?"

"I can hear you," I say. My arms prickle with goose bumps. Whispering makes me think of wool that you are rubbing on your tongue. I want to spit but I can't, because it would just land on me.

"Um, OK," Kandy says. "We've got to go." She says it like she's leaving a conversation, as if it's yesterday afternoon and we're talking on the phone and I'm just going to sit here with the telephone pressed against my ear, waiting for her to come back. We have a landline now. Mom gave up her cell phone. It's like we didn't just move, we traveled back through time to 1975. In the kitchen, there's a patterned, squishy floor with gold flecks. There's a spot where you can sit where the sun comes in the window and makes a rectangle of sparkling light on the floor. That's where I was sitting yesterday, tracing patterns on the gold bits, when Kandy called to say that I could join her club if I passed the *initiation*.

This is the initiation.

I guess I'm not going to pass.

The heads disappear again. My own head hurts.

My own head wants to disappear into the warm sunshininess of the Texan blue sky, to melt in the heat like a candle in a flame. But instead, my head's an ice cube, shivering and clattering away on top of my neck, my teeth rattling from the cold. My ears are ringing like they did after the Rory Devon concert that Maria Potts' parents took ten of us to for her birthday last May. Rory was so amazing. We were in the front row and we could see the sweat on his face. We could even feel it freckling our own faces like a creepy but awesome drizzle when he danced. It was basically the last time in my life that I was truly happy, even if for three days afterwards, my ears wouldn't stop ringing. I didn't shower for a week.

I swallow down some more crying and nearly choke to death on my own spit, which would actually be a sort of ironic way to die in a well, if *ironic* means what I think it means, which is "so pathetic that it's almost funny, but is actually tragic."

A bunch of pebbles and loose dirt come raining down onto my face and shoulders. Mandy's face appears. "Oh! You're still there," she deadpans, like maybe while they were gone, I just climbed out and went home.

"Yes, I am," I say. Where else would I be? I sneeze three more times. I can't not sneeze in groups of three. It's a thing of mine. But there is not enough room in here to both breathe and sneeze. My eyes hurt, my nose hurts, my throat hurts, and my lungs hurt, like I'm really for sure going to have an asthma attack and die.

"We've been talking and we've decided that . . . well, just get out of there," says Mandy, like that's it. It's up to me.

"HOW?" I yell. "I don't know HOW! I can't. I CAN'T."

"Wiggle," Mandy says impatiently, leaning in so far that I can smell the perfume that she says she stole from Walgreens. I bet she just took it from her mom's bathroom. It smells like something too sweet combined with cough medicine. Then her gum falls out of her mouth and lands in my hair. IN MY HAIR. I can't reach it, for obvious reasons. "My gum! Oopsy!" She laughs. "So, um, wiggle back up now."

"Wiggle *up*?" says Sandy, and then she giggles. "Did you just spit your gum on her?"

The gum smells like spearmint and drool. I can see it out of the corner of my eye, sitting there above my left eye on a crooked overhang of bangs. Mandy yelps with laughter. Then I hear, "What?" Then I hear, "In her *hair*." Then I hear Kandy's manic bellow of laughter. She roars like nothing has ever been funny before and this is the funniest thing that humanity will ever achieve. I'm glad none of them have phones because if they did, they'd be filming this and turning it into something that goes viral on the Internet and the whole world would be laughing at me at the same time. Gum in her hair! Hold me! OMG! So funny! LOL

I try to ignore them. I'm the one in the snake-filled well with a gob of spitty spearmint gunk in my hair. I *wiggle*. I hold my breath and squish my arms in even tighter and I move my hips back and forth, just a bit, because just a bit is all I can do. As it turns out, wiggling is a bad idea because my body doesn't wiggle up, it slides down.

And down.

And down.

How deep is this well?

I think I'm screaming, but I might not be screaming. I might be holding my breath. I might be dead. I might be sleeping somewhere in New Jersey, in my old water bed, and any second now, I'll wake up and everything will have been a dream. A terrible dream. Texas. Mandy, Kandy, and Sandy. The well.

All of it.

When I come to a stop, I'm shaking all over. I hope I don't shake myself loose and fall farther still. When I first crashed down here, I was close enough to the sky to feel like I could maybe, just about almost possibly somehow climb out. Now I'm not even close. The sky-hole is so far away it looks as tiny as a saucer, and I am way bigger than a teacup.

"Help," I whimper, even though I know there is no way they can hear me without shouting. Not now.

The skin on my elbows and knees has rubbed off on the well walls. I am raw. I feel as pinkish red as a lump of ground raw meat. All of my skin hurts and burns like a bad sunburn that's been scraped dry by a sandpapery towel.

"Please help," I say.

"ARE YOU AT THE BOTTOM OF THE WELL?" one of The Girls yells.

"No!" I answer. "I mean, I don't know! No. I guess not."

I wish I could see down. I wish I could see the bottom to know how much farther I might go, how much more air is under my feet before they might finally touch down on something solid, something real, something to hold me up.

2

Erased

I can't see myself at all, partly because it is dark in the well and partly because I can look up and I can look straight ahead, but the rest of my body is all stuffed down below my shoulders like a sausage in a skin. I feel as if I've been erased from the neck down, like my body is not really here with me. I'm just a head, alone. My body is separate from me, but it can still send me messages. Messages like *OUCH*. All the parts that hurt, all the parts that are dangling, all the parts that are wedged, those parts are all messaging me at the same time so that my brain just feels white, fuzzy, painful noise.

I take a deep breath and hold it, and it feels like a whole army of tiny samurai soldiers are stabbing into my non-existent sides. I can feel it, but at the same time, it feels like it isn't happening to me. When I shift my weight, my leg throbs like a giant heart, sending the pain up through my veins. My body is the Internet and my brain is my e-mail and it's receiving the news. *Ouch, ouch, ouch.* Love, mylegs@therestofmybody.com, e-mailing me from the black nothing below.

Black, like a black hole, like we learned about in science, just waiting to pull everything in and unravel it into a backward explosion. I don't get how that works, how things can *implode*, but I didn't put up my hand to ask. At school, I'm invisible. It's part of the plan. I didn't want anyone to really notice me until I was part of the Mandy, Kandy, Sandy alliance. Until I was safe, in a group of friends. Until I was one of The Girls.

Ha. *Ha.*

I'm such an *idiot*.

I should have picked someone else. Anyone else. That kid with the purple glasses! That girl with the birthmark that leaks down her face onto her neck! The BFFs who wear their long blond hair in matching headbands every day! I could have made that work. I could have been whoever they wanted me to be, I guess.

But now, where am I? Down a well. Totally alone. In the dark.

Some pretty bad things that have happened to me in the dark include: 1. Accidentally stepping on our old dog, Hayfield, and breaking his back leg. 2. Slipping down the stairs when I took a wrong turn to the bathroom at a sleepover at Molly Fortin's house in second grade. 3. Being stuck in a well.

"Where are you?" I yell. "YOU GUYS. Don't leave me!"

"Don't get hysterical!" says Sandy. I have to stretch my hearing to the max to even catch what she's saying. Her now-tiny face blocks the distant light for a second. Then it disappears. I blink and blink. My eyes are starting to adjust. My heart slows back down a tiny bit. I can see the well wall. I can see the outline of bricks.

"Help!" I yell again. "HELP HELP HELP HELP HELP."

"Stop yelling!" yells Kandy, appearing, her teeth shining like tiny flashlights. We ARE helping. DUH!" She's starting to sound a whole lot less caring and a whole bunch more annoyed, like this is something I've done to her, like I've really inconvenienced her. My insides curl up and pinch.

"I can see your teeth!" I yell.

"No kidding," she says, and disappears again.

Then Sandy appears, scowls, and vanishes. I wish Sandy was the one who had fallen down the well. I wish *she* was the one who was small enough to fit. Or maybe I just wish another well would open up next to this one and she would go shooting down it like a waterslide and land in the big ball of lava in the center of the earth, or maybe past that, maybe in China.

If I could actually fall that far, it might be pretty

cool, if only the tunnel was just a bit wider and smooth as marble and all my skin didn't get rubbed off on the way. No one welcomes a kid without skin when they suddenly pop up in the middle of a busy intersection in Shanghai or someplace else that is Chinese. They'd probably scream. They'd probably run. Maybe they'd think I was a ghost or a monster, risen from the sewers. If a Chinese person with no skin suddenly fell up here and appeared from the sewer at the corner of Main and First, the people in this podunk town wouldn't exactly be giving them a warm hug and a Dr. Pepper. They'd call the sheriff. They'd have that person in the slammer before you could say, "Are you OK?" You'd have people calling CNN, posting that an alien had landed, taking selfies with the poor thing. Someone would declare that the zombie apocalypse had started. And then, before you knew it, the whole town would probably drive to Dallas in a mass evacuation, in their big dusty pickup trucks, kids hanging out of the back with hunting rifles, ready to shoot the undead.

I can't hear the girls anymore so I remind them I am here by yelling some more. My voice is getting tired and heavy, and trying to use it is like trying to lob a bowling ball uphill. I can't hear their voices but I'm sure I can still hear giggling. "It's not funny!" I say, but they must think it is because they don't stop. "I'm bleeding!" I shout, my voice as scratchy as an old smoker's. "I'm scared," I add in a quieter voice. I'm glad they can't hear me because admitting it would just make them laugh harder. Mom once told me that I take everything too seriously, and maybe this is one of those things. Maybe it is funny? I force a laugh, but the thing is, it isn't funny. Not even a bit.

"Oh, sorry!" says Mandy, suddenly face-first back in the hole, her braid hanging down like Rapunzel's, just like Kandy's did before, but nowhere even close enough to reach. Mandy has the longest hair. She has never had her hair cut. Not even once. When she sits down, she can tuck the end of it under her butt. "We were just talking about, like, something else? You know? But now we're going to save you!"

"Kandy," I say. "I mean, *Mandy*. Come on! HURRY! I'm going to die!"

"It's AMANDA," she says, snottily, before disappearing again. "We told you, you have to be in the club to call us by our *good* names."

I don't think I've ever hated anyone as much as I hate her right now, and that's the truth.

"Grrr," I say, low down in my throat, but the vibration makes my ribs hurt, so I stop.

It smells bad down here, like farts and rotting fruit. I remember hearing once that even if you've never smelled something dead, when you do smell something dead, you know right away and will say to yourself, "Oh, *that* is the smell of something dead!" Like it's programmed into our cells to recognize death. Well, *I* smell something dead. There is something dead underneath me, somewhere between me and China. Maybe the dead thing is the last person who fell down the well, the last person who tried to join their stupid club and stood on the board to sing the national anthem. Maybe the whole well is full of dead kids! My heart starts to pound really hard.

"Seriously, hurry!" I yell. "You guys have to get me out! There's something dead in here!"

"What is it?" Kandy yells, like it matters.

"I don't know," I shout. "I can't see anything."

"Is it a zombie?" Sandy says, unhelpfully.

"That is NOT FUNNY," I yell.

"Calm down," calls Amanda in a sing-songy voice. Then, "BOOO!" Her laugh echoes around me. I want to plug my ears so bad, but I can't. I can't do anything but listen. "BOOO!" she can hardly even say it, she's laughing too hard.

I've decided now for sure that Amanda is my least favorite. She has red hair and white skin, and freckles crawl all over her face like amoebas. Her teeth look like Chiclets wedged crookedly into her gums, or they would if she brushed them often enough to keep them white. Sandra (Sandy!) is blonde and has braces already because her uncle is an orthodontist. Kandy is a brunette. (No one calls Kandy anything except Kandy. I don't even know what else to call her!) Her teeth are totally perfect naturally. Everything about how she looks is totally perfect naturally. That's why she makes all the big decisions. She's the leader. I didn't even know them yet when I figured that out. You can just tell. It's something about the way she walks and the way she dresses and the way the other girls are trying to walk like her and dress like her, but they aren't quite as good at it. They just look like imitation-Kandy, not the real thing. They look like they want so bad to be the real thing that they would do anything, like sell their soul to the Devil maybe, if he made those kinds of deals.

Like drop the new kid down the well, even.

And laugh about it.

I said they were the popular girls, but I left out the part where they are also the meanest girls in the whole sixth grade. But, obviously, popular and mean are tied together so tight they're like those knots that just tighten and tighten no matter how hard you try to untangle them. Mean is where they get their power. The thing with mean girls is that everyone knows that if you aren't one of them, they're going to destroy you, tiny bit by tiny bit. And I'm not going to lie, I've been destroyed enough for this year, for this whole life even.

When you move somewhere new, you get to *be* someone new. I was ready. What was left of me was ready to be Kammie Summers, Mean Girl #4.

I didn't have anything to lose.

"Kandy!" I yell. "Get a rope! Pull me out!"

She leans into the well again. The opening is a whole lot bigger at the top than at the part where I am wedged. The well gets narrower as it descends. For a second, she looks so friendly up there that I remember why I like her. She's so pretty! She's so normal! She's so happy! She's never had so many bad things happen to her at once that she's done the worst thing you can do. She's never been broken and sloppily put back together with paste and scars.

"There's no rope," Kandy yells, and at first

I think she's said, "There's no hope," which also sounds true. "Stop screaming!" she adds. "I can't think. I'm, like, trying really hard to think of something, you know." Then, "Ew, it *stinks* in here. We'll have to just . . . go get someone, I guess. Stay there."

"Where else would I go?" I yell back weakly, but she's already disappeared from view. And then, just like that, I hear the whisper-crunch sound of their feet stepping away from me, leaving me alone. It's as if all the sound has been sucked away with them, into a vacuum. "Implode," I whisper. This is what it sounds like in outer space, I'll bet, your ears filled up with its emptiness, nothing but the whole universe all around you. We just learned in science class that space is a vacuum, but if that's true, then why aren't we all sucked clean away? Or, at the very least, why can't I be sucked up out of this well? Why doesn't gravity push us up instead of pulling us down?

Kandy is probably shaking out her hair while she runs in her slightly gallop-y way, trying to get the well-smell off her. In my head, this happens in slow motion, the sun throwing a shower of golden sparkles into her hair, which is maybe now freed from its braid, bouncing perfectly like in a shampoo commercial.

I wonder how long it will take *me* to get clean after this. I'll probably never be clean again. Ten years from now, I'll scratch my ear and dust will fall out. If I live that long, I guess. We don't even have a bathtub in our new place, only a really terrible, rust-dripping shower that smells like cat pee and broken hearts. I used to love to take baths with a million bubbles, so many that they were like a blanket that I could hide under. My favorite bubbles smelled like chewing gum and had a pink girl on the bottle. She had boobs the size of watermelons and her face was permanently frozen in a half-creepy smile, but the bubbles smelled like happiness and birthday parties and dancing and vanilla cake and everything good.

I guess the bank reclaimed those bubbles, too. I hope those bankers love them. I hope they go home and take off their expensive-looking blue shirts and striped ties and then climb into a bath full of sweet pink bubbles. I hope they say to themselves, "Gosh, I'm so great! I stole these from an 11-year-old girl who never did anything wrong. I'm a good guy! Love these bubbles!"

Jerks.

I hope they get a rash.

In the dark, I am starting to see things like underwater coral and moving shapes that I know aren't really there; they are just shadows on my eyeballs or things floating past my retinas. I blink hard. Staring at the hole where the light shines in has left a stamp on my eyes, so even if I close them, I see a round, lighter patch that's still out of reach, even though it's *there* on my eyelid. It's inside me, but I'll never reach it, like how stuff in 3-D movies can look real enough to touch. That sounds like a metaphor for something important, but I don't really get what it is. Metaphors and similes make my head hurt, picking apart those sentences in Language Arts, making all those words fall away from their sentences and separating them into gerunds and modifiers and whatevers. It's like sentence massacres, those poor words bleeding sadly all over the page. I don't know why school has to take everything good and turn it boring and painful and bad. If I ran a school, I'd make it fun. I'd make it better. I don't know how, but I would.

Speaking of bleeding, my leg is wet and kind of sticky, and I just know that's blood, coagulating down there. Gross. Even the word *coagulating* is gross. It's a word that coagulates in your throat when you whisper it in the dark. "Coagulating," I whisper, then I cough hard, clearing it away.

Anyway, I wish I hadn't worn these shorts, my favorites, cutoffs that are the exact perfect length and don't gape out at the waist, like most jeans do on me. I bet they are ruined. I bet holes tore right through them while I was falling. I'll have to throw them out. I'll never get another pair. We just don't have money for that anymore, and shorts this good don't show up at the Goodwill.

Once they found out that we shop at the Goodwill, The Girls would've kicked me out anyway.

I should never have tried to join Kandy's stupid, awful club. It's ruined everything. I might even die! I thought I was going to be someone different here in Texas. I thought I was going to be someone tough and happy and sparkly and untouchable, like they are. I thought I could do that, just start over in a different way.

I was wrong.

Mom would say, "Oh, honey, those girls aren't your people." And I know it. I knew it all along. But Mom isn't exactly around much now to give advice, and I didn't ask anyway. I didn't have to ask. I knew—I just didn't care. Or maybe I wanted new people.

My people would never have laughed at me. Not even Tracy Kelliher. Not even after she stopped talking to me. She was never that kind of mean. Not Mandy-mean. Not let-me-fall-down-a-well mean. Not even close to that. Their meanness is multiplied by three because it's like if one person feels a certain way, then automatically the other two do, too. They are practically the same girl, but times three. Three times better. Three times prettier. Three times meaner. Kandy, Amanda, and Sandra. Kandy, Mandy, and Sandy. At first, I wished my name could be shortened to something that ends with an _andy, but now I'm glad it's not.

It took me five whole days to work up the nerve to go up to Kandy at recess and say, "Can I hang out with you guys?" I practiced first, trying to make it sound like I didn't care, like I was tougher and cooler than her. When I finally said it, I stared at a tree behind her, watching a bird hop from one branch to another. Scrunched my juice box up in my hand, casually tossed it in the garbage can behind her. Kept my eyes off her face. The bird was small and brown. The juice box went into the can like a three-pointer in basketball. I swept my hair out of my eyes. I was busy and this was just a question and it wasn't the most important thing I'd ever asked anyone, like I didn't stay awake all night the night before, practicing the ask.

Out of the corner of my eye, I watched as she looked at me, up and down really slowly, and said,

"Soooooorry, but we're all full. Like, you know, we have a blonde. A brunette. And a redhead." As if it was obvious that all clubs had one girl with each hair color.

"You don't have a black girl," I drawled back, improvising, talking slowly and deliberately.

Kandy said, "You aren't black!" Her eyes widened. Then she looked suspicious.

"That's true," I said. "But my grandmother on my mom's side was." I made that up, but Kandy didn't know anything about me yet. I squinted up at the sun.

"You're just another brunette," said Kandy. "And we don't *really* have room for you." But I could tell she was hesitating.

"Please?" I said.

If I could go back in time and erase anything, it would be that *please*. I showed weakness. I could tell by the way her back straightened up and she stared me down. She sucked all the power back from me through her eyes. Then she giggled.

I should have walked away and started hanging

out with someone else. There were plenty of kids who wanted to be with me! I was the new girl! The mysterious new girl! Or I could have done what I got good at in my old school, which is to pretend to be really into my book and to not look up until the bell rang to go back inside. To be a secret inside myself. To stay away from everyone and anyone who could hurt me.

I could have kept myself safe that way.

But I *wanted*. I totally wanted to be with them. To *be* them. It's so lame, now that I think about it. It's so dumb. *I'm* so dumb to have ever wanted anything to do with them.

But I couldn't help it.

It had to do with the way they moved through the school like sharks, and the other students moved to the side. The way the kids stared at the three of them, like they were movie stars or just famous for being famous. And they have this clubhouse—an actual *clubhouse*, like in a movie or a book—that is to die for. Amanda's dad had built it just for them, in their yard, right out front so everyone could see it. Her house was on the small hill behind the school, so no one could miss it, perched up there like it was special, the most special house in town.

Inside the clubhouse, there was real furniture and curtains and a white shag rug and even an Internet connection so they could watch movies in there on the Xbox. Out front, there were three chairs painted in different colors, one for each of them, and a pot of geraniums the color of fireworks. It had everything. I wanted to live in that club-house. I wanted to put my posters of Rory on the walls. I wanted to lie on the bed in there and read Harry Potter books over and over again and never ever have to leave.

"Maybe you can be the one with short hair," Sandra said. "Like, um, we've already got a normal blonde, brunette, and redhead. I mean, I *guess* you can. If you have to join." She looked at Kandy. "What?" Sandy said. "She could pull it off! She's, you know." Sandy smirked. "Boyish." She shrugged. "I'm just saying."

"I can do that," I said.

I don't know why I said that. My hair was the only thing in my life that was any good. It came down to my shoulders and I could make it do loose curls without even really trying. I could make it look like I'd spent the day at the beach. I could straighten it and make it shine like a crow's feathers. I could do any kind of braid you can even make up. I was good at braiding. Maybe even better than they were.

"Really?" Sandy said. "OK. Good! Great. It will be, like, your test. *Part* of it. We'll have other tests. But the first one is cutting your hair. Mandy will do it. She's awesome at hair cutting and stuff like that."

I should have known that their stupid club was going to land me exactly where I am, about to die in a well with a terrible haircut that Amanda did with her mom's kitchen scissors, the blades all sticky from who-knows-what, little patches of rust changing the usual *snip-snip* scissor noise to something more like Styrofoam rubbing against itself. Amanda, who had *never* had a haircut herself, not

ever, like that made her a better person than everyone else. Why did I think *she* could do it? When she
started cutting, I wasn't scared. Not really. It felt
OK, the weight of my hair falling in clumps onto
her kitchen floor. The other girls were oohing and
aahing. "You are soooooo talented," Kandy said.
"You could be a hairdresser when you grow up! You
totally should do that."

"Maybe even for movie stars," said Sandy.

"Maybe even for Talia," said Mandy.

The girls sighed. They loved Talia. She was their
favorite singer, but I didn't like her. She was too big.
Not big, like fat or tall, but *big*, like *in your face*. I
like people who stay gently where they are, a little
bit behind what they are doing. They just *sing*. You
think of the song first, because it's so good, before
you think of the person doing the singing. And then
you find yourself looking at them because they are
so good at the thing they are doing, not because
they are flapping their tongue in your face and
screaming and all half-naked and stuff. Too much.

When I grow up, I'm going to be one of the *gently*

present people. (Grandma used to say that it was better to be gently present than to announce yourself, and I know exactly what she meant by that. Talia could have used a few lessons from Grandma, that's for sure.) I'm going to be someone who makes you look, slowly, over to where I am. I mean, if I ever turn out to be good at anything.

I felt pretty, the way they were staring at me when they cut my hair. But now that I think of it, it was like I was showing off, sitting there letting them hack off all my hair. *I* was Talia. *I* was being bigger than I am, all LOOK AT ME. IN YOUR FACE. But I liked it. That's the confusing part. I liked that they were looking. I guess I have a bit of Talia in me, after all. I guess that's another bit of me that I don't like so much.

Grandma wouldn't like it either.

After it was done, I got up from that stool and I felt lighter, better, prettier. But then I *looked*. I saw myself in the bathroom mirror, and I almost threw up my peanut butter and jelly sandwich all over the sink, which had toothpaste spit clumped by the drain. I swallowed just in time. In the mirror, I looked pale and sick and weirdly exposed. Hairless, like some kind of newborn animal that should be cute but isn't. My freckles stood out on my white skin like flecks of blood on paper. My bangs were so high up on my forehead that I looked like someone who had just got some super-surprising news. There were clumps and bits of hair sticking out and even one patch above my ear that looked bald.

"Wow," I lied. "It's so awesome and, like, sick." I'd never said that word out loud before to mean "good," and it felt dumb and wrong in my mouth. But then again, my hair looked dumb and wrong on my head. I looked dumb and wrong in the mirror. And everything about my life was totally dumb. And totally wrong. And totally sick, not in a good way.

I forced a grin at myself in the glass, which didn't make me look happy, it just made me look crazy. I made my smile look real by crinkling my eye corners. "Smize," like that woman on TV always says. "Smile with your eyes." My eyes stung with tears.

"I love it," I said again and I *almost* believed me. I loved the way it felt, that wasn't a lie. My head was so light. Without hair, I kind of did feel like a boy, strong and wiry, in some way I hadn't known before. "I'll fix it at home," I said when Amanda tried to smooth down a cowlick on my crown with her palm, like my head was suddenly her property, OK for her to touch. I dodged out from under her hand. "I know how," I lied. "I have good hair . . . stuff." I rubbed my fingers along the soft fraying at the hem of my shorts. It made me feel safe, like I was still me, standing there in my favorite shorts.

I pulled my socks up to my knees and stood up. "What's next?" I said, grinning, like I was having fun and not like I was about to puke or faint or both. I pretended not to see Kandy and Sandy whispering to each other. I pretended not to notice how they were giggling.

I bet my socks are now covered with blood. I

can't see them, but they must still be there. I bet they are filthy and wrecked.

Everything is filthy and wrecked.

My shorts, my socks, me. My so-called life.

I try hard to not cry again. What's the point? Mom's a crier and it never got her anywhere. When those girls cut my hair, my biggest worry (other than how awful I looked) was how hard Mom would cry when she saw it. "Your hair," she'd say. "What did you do?" She *loved* my hair. Even now that she was working all the time and could barely stay awake when she wasn't, she liked to brush my hair while we watched TV together, me leaning back on the couch and her standing behind, brushing and brushing and brushing. We haven't watched anything for a while, actually. We haven't done it since we moved here. We haven't seen a single episode of our favorite show, *The Singer*, since Dad went to prison. Maybe it's not even on anymore. I wanted to ask The Girls, but I thought they'd laugh at me. Maybe watching *The Singer* isn't cool anymore either.

"Here," Kandy said. She reached over and sprayed something onto my head. Right away, my lungs almost slammed shut. I gasped and coughed.

"It's just hairspray," she laughed. "Settle down."

The hairspray smelled like plastic and disinfectant, like everything I've ever regretted doing, like that time I put salt in Robby's Coke as a joke but I used too much. I didn't know that he was going to just gulp it down in one swallow like that. Who does that? Anyway, he drank it all and had to go to the hospital because something bad happened to his kidneys. I knew I was the worst person in the world when he was loaded into the back of the ambulance and his skin was the color of snow. The smell of the hospital made me gag and he said, "Stop making this about you!" and his eyes were all red from crying and I was so embarrassed and sad for both of us that I pretended to get mad and I ran out to the parking lot and waited by the car for Mom and Dad to finally come out. Robby had to stay the night.

"Oh, ooops," Kandy shrieked. "That's not hair-spray! It's, um, cleaner stuff. Lysol? Is that for toilets? Ha ha! Sorry!"

I shrugged, like it didn't matter. And I guess it didn't.

None of that matters now.

Now I'm stuck in a well. And if Mom finds out about *this*, I'm pretty sure that she's going to be so brokenhearted that she'll collapse. She might not be able to stop crying, not if she starts for real. She's been holding it in for a while now, come to think of it. She hasn't cried at all since we moved to Texas. And if *I'm* the one who breaks her down, I will die. I won't be able to stand it. On the bright side, if I'm dead, I guess she won't be so disappointed about my hair.

She'll just be sad, period.

Sometimes I feel like Mom has all this stuff in a big bag she has to carry around—everything about Dad and Texas and her two jobs and us—and she has to be brave about it. But just putting one more thing in it will make her drop it, and it could crush her completely, like in a cartoon. She'll be as flat as a piece of paper, freckled with a sprinkling of blood.

And it will be my fault.

But at least I won't know about it, if I'm dead and all that.

3

Alone

I think about crying some more, but I decide not to. There's no one close enough to hear it, for one thing. If a girl cries in a well and no one hears it, is she really crying? That sounds like a question that Dad's only friend, our old neighbor Mr. Thacker, would ask and then I'd have to think about the answer for a long time and we'd talk about it over a big plate of fried fish. He said he liked talking to me. He said our philosophies were the same. I didn't know what he meant, but he was OK. I liked it when he came over. He'd talk and I'd listen and watch the long hairs in his nose move when he got really excited, like cat whiskers. When he started to shout, they got especially wild, brawling in his nostrils. Sometimes he made me do all the talking. I didn't have nose hair though, so it wasn't the same. When I got excited, I just waved my hands around more. Once I knocked over the whole plate of that fish. Hayfield was the happiest he'd ever been.

Mr. Thacker and I already answered, "If a tree falls in the forest and no one is around to hear it, does it make a noise?" We talked about that one a lot, him shouting and whisker-waving, me not-shouting and waving my hands. I could tell he thought I was smart. Sometimes after I talked to Mr. Thacker, I *felt* smart. I felt like even my blood thrumming through my veins was smarter, like he'd cracked open my cells and poured in something extra intelligent. We decided that of course the tree would make noise. Did the person who asked the question ever go into the forest? Forests are full of animals and birds and stuff. Just because there's no person there to hear something doesn't mean that *nothing* heard it. Something is always alive in the woods. Humans really do think they are soooooo special, like hearing a tree falling over makes it so. I said that and Mr. Thacker agreed. He said that he wished his students thought about things from the same angles that I thought of them. I said, "You mean from really low down because I'm so small?" And he laughed, which made me feel both funny and smart. In other words, it was the best.

Mr. Thacker was always coming over to talk, bringing those plates of fried fish. He said fish would make me grow tall and strong. I don't know what kind of fish it was. Mostly I ate it to be polite. I certainly didn't grow. The truth is, I don't care any more for eating fish than looking at them. Mr. Thacker also said his students were a new breed of hippies. Hippies who listen to bad music, he said, and laughed. It was weird because Dad always called Mr. Thacker a hippie and when I asked why, he shrugged and said, "long hair, guitar-strumming, overthinker." The new ones, I guess, aren't like that.

The man who runs the music store in No-wheresville is a long-haired, guitar-strumming overthinker, too. He's younger than Mr. Thacker. I wonder what Mr. Thacker would say about Dave. He listens to *good* music. He says I have good taste, music-wise. He says that it doesn't matter what you listen to, as long as it moves you inside, that it's not about being cool or doing what everyone else does, it's about what makes you *feel*. He says that music is poetry that has a tune that you hear with your soul. I guess I like those deep-thinking hippies, too, who make me feel like more than I am. People like Mr. Thacker and Record Store Dave.

Anyway, if Mr. Thacker was here, I bet he could deeply think of a way to get me out of this well.

I think Mr. Thacker is right about most things, but wrong about this one thing we talked about once, which was whether or not all people see colors the same way. He said no, or at least that we couldn't know. I think we can know. I mean, we all know that a carrot is orange. The weird thing is that when you ask someone that question, if all people see colors the same way, then you say, "Think of orange, for example," almost everyone thinks of a carrot. Like carrots are the only orange thing. It's like they have a universal orangeness that everyone just understands, without thinking about it.

The air in this well is orange. The air in this well is a carrot. But not a real one, a super dried out one, one that's shriveled in the bottom of the vegetable drawer for months before anyone notices it down there, looking like a mummy's old finger.

It sounds like my breaths are scraping in and out against the walls, like I'm breathing out not carbon dioxide, but broken glass. One time Robby threw a glass of milk at me in the kitchen, the whole glass, and it flew through the air, whistled past my face, and smashed against the wall. We were both super surprised by that even though he had said he was going to throw it and we both know that glass breaks. I helped him pick up all the pieces before Mom and Dad saw. One shard slipped cleanly into the skin on my thumb and made a perfect letter J. I wrapped it in a Band-Aid. It was only afterward that it started to hurt. The hurt was so deep, it felt like it was aching in my bone. That's how my lungs feel now, cut like that.

I'm glad I can't see my knees in the dark. I know they are skinned. They burn and sting. Skinned knees are always worst when you see them for the first time, with their hanging-off skin and your very own blood dribbling out of you in red ribbons. When I learned how to ride a bike, it was Robby who showed me how. It was Robby who held the seat while I pedaled furiously. It was Robby who let go and left me flying down the hill, before I ended in a terrible knee-first crash that left my knees permanently scarred. I wonder if the well wall has scraped that scar right off. I wonder if I'll get a new scar or if my skin will just give up and stay open, the shiny white saucer of my kneecap glowing there for all the world to see.

I guess that story makes it seem like I'd be mad at Robby for that, but I wasn't mad. Mom would never have let go, she'd never have had the nerve. And Dad? Well, Dad wasn't much into teaching kids how to ride bikes, I guess. Dad didn't seem to want the chance. But Robby did. Robby used to always be there for me, for stuff like that. All the spaces Dad left unfilled, he just stepped into. Dad's always been leaving spaces unfilled. He tried to fill them with nice presents and junk we didn't need. Now he's left too big of a space to even try to fill at all. At least, he doesn't try. He doesn't even send e-mails. I check at the school library and my account, kammiethephilosopher@gmail.com, just keeps filling up with junk mail and group e-mails to all the kids who used to take skating classes at the arena uptown. Reading those skating e-mails makes me miss home like an ache.

Speaking of aches, my legs are cramping like growing pains but worse. I usually like growing pains, not because I'm a freak, but because I like the *fact* of them, the proof that I'm actually growing, even when it happens for me in the slowest of slow motion and sometimes not at all. We used to have a measuring wall where we wrote the date and made a mark for our heights. Robby's was an inch away from the last mark each time, but mine got all crammed together, all my measuring dates sharing that same tiny inch. I don't miss that. It was just a reminder of how I wasn't any good at growing, no matter how hard I tried, no matter how long I hung upside down hoping gravity would help.

I try to relax and breathe and not think, which somehow makes me slide farther down and down, as if relaxing shrinks me like Alice in the Alice in Wonderland movie. I scrabble at the walls as much as I can with my arms still stuck against my sides. My fingertips sting. Maybe after this, I won't have fingerprints. I'll be smooth all over, like the fresh skin you get under a scab.

My arms are as useless as seal flippers, which wouldn't be so useless if I was actually a seal, but I'm not, thank goodness. I mean, think of all those fish I'd have to see in that scenario.

I slide a little bit more. Then more.

What if? I think. What if? What if this is forever? What if this well has no bottom?

What if I *die*?

"Help!" I say. I know no one is there. *I'm* the tree in the forest, falling and falling, and I can't even prove that I'm here. This is Texas, so it's pretty much been abandoned by the animals even. It's too hot. So with no one listening, maybe I didn't make a sound. Maybe I don't exist, after all.

I slide a tiny bit more.

I'm going to die in a well.

My heart speeds up, squishing blood through its chambers so fast that it might just collapse and burst, like that might fuel me up and out of here. I cry harder, which hurts more and more—my lungs, my skinned knees, my eyes, everywhere.

I hurt, so I must be here.

I must exist.

I should have introduced myself to the *nice* girls. The freaks and weirdos. Mom always said that weirdos were the best people. "Fly your freak flag high," she'd say. "Find your people."

"But *I'm* not a freak," I'd say.

And she'd laugh and say, "Sure you are, honey, we all are. Some of us just know that better than others."

"You're wrong," I'd say. "You're weird. *You're* a freak. But me? I'm normal. I'm not *you*."

"No," she'd say. "You're not me. If you were, you'd know that 'weird' is better. 'Weird' is the best."

"Don't worry," Robby would say. "Kammie's the biggest freak of them all."

Then I'd throw a punch. That's the thing with Robby: He's big and strong but I'm fast. If I can land a blow before he knows it's coming, it's basically the same as winning.

But the dumb thing is that Mom was right. Again. I should've looked to see who was wearing the worst-fitting clothes, which kid had the ugliest hair or the worst crooked teeth, or maybe the one with the awkward walk. I bet those kids would have been kind. I bet they never would have said, "Sing a song on this rotting board that's covering an old well!" I bet they never would have laughed when I fell.

I wonder if Heaven is real. I hope so. If it's not, this whole life is going to have felt like a major rip off. "God?" I say, "sorry for everything I ever thought or did that was bad, like that thing with the salt."

I slide a few more inches, my peeled-back skin rubbing even more on the gritty wall. I'm being peeled. I'm *meat*. Or a potato.

"Shit," I swear. I'm not allowed to swear, so I never have, but now is as good a time as any to start. The *shit* feels strong and like I really mean it. "This is shit," I say, my voice shaking like a baby's. Crying again, still crying.

Then finally, my foot sticks on something that's poking through the well wall, a rock maybe or a really deep tree root. It makes me feel SO MUCH better, having that place to stand. I'm saved. I'm saved! I murmur thanks to God, just in case it was Him who did it. If not, it doesn't hurt to say it, right?

"Glory, glory, hallelujah!" I sing and my voice echoes in a muffled hum. It's pretty much the only hymn-like thing I know, outside of Christmas songs. We aren't religious. Dad says God is dead. I don't know if he's right. He read it on a T-shirt one day when we were on the train going into the city and acted like it was a message from God himself. But God wouldn't send messages if he was dead, so I just rolled my eyes and ignored him and looked out the window at New Jersey whooshing by. The thing is, if God is dead, who is looking after us? Not *Dad*, that's for sure. I'm going to go out on a limb here and say that God is better at message-sending than Dad is, and God doesn't even have an e-mail address.

"I'm OK," I say out loud. It comes out thick. My throat is also shrinking, along with the rest of me. My throat is a well and the words are me. Stuck. "I'm stuck," I say, then I stop, because it hurts. I try to bend myself so that I'm more comfortable, but wells just aren't built for comfort, not like new cars or couches or water beds.

I had a water bed at our old house. I loved how it sloshed underneath me when I rolled over. I miss that bed, except for when it used to leak and I'd wake up screaming from bad dreams where fish were brushing by my legs with their spiky fins and hungry mouths. Robby thought that bed was hilarious. "Hey, Kammie," he'd say. "1980 called! It wants its bed back."

"So funny," I'd say. "So funny that I forgot to laugh."

Then he'd come and lie next to me on that bed. He'd slam his body up and down to make waves and I'd giggle until I thought I'd pee my pants. It was more fun than it sounds.

The bed was Mom's bed in college. When I closed my eyes on that bed, I'd imagine what it was like to be her, living alone, moving to a new state all by herself, starting her real life. I'd wonder how much she cried on that bed, missing Grandma. Grandma may have been an old liar, but she was pretty nice to be around. I bet she was a good mom. She sure made good cookies.

I was more than a little sad to leave that bed behind. "It's just a bed," Mom said, but she was wrong. It was more than that.

Besides, even if we *could* afford it, they don't

make water beds like that anymore. They just stopped existing, at least for now. But maybe they'll be like the old vinyl records that hipsters love. (I love the word hipster because it's basically just like hippie, but newer and better and with blacker glasses and tidier beards.) Hippies are hipsters now but records are still the same old big, flat, black plastic discs that Dad had a collection of and nothing to play them on, that we weren't allowed to touch, not ever. I guess we left those behind, too. Well, Dad deserves that.

I tip my head up and take a deep breath and hold it. I imagine that a piece of the blue sky and the wispy white clouds floating by are pulled into my lungs, that it's blue inside me somehow. A fading blue, but warm. Above my well-top window, there is a tree. The wind keeps pushing the branch back and forth. I don't know what kind of tree it is. I'm not good at that kind of stuff. Nature is dirty and there is way too much nature around here. It's the kind with leaves, small, dusty-looking ones. I try to think of that shadowy branch as a loving arm that's reaching over to save me, but it isn't and I'm scared.

I'm so scared.

When I was little, I used to sleep with this stuffed cat named Ratty Catty. I would do just about anything to have Ratty Catty right now, tucked up under my chin, smelling like me and something else, something warm. Something safe. Smelling like a place where I haven't been for a long time and can barely even really remember.

Thinking about being scared makes me scareder still and I wish one of the girls had stayed up there, and what if they don't tell anyone after all, and what if they leave me here to die and go home to watch TV instead? Maybe right now they are perched on their couches, in front of TV tables, swallowing forkfuls of barbecued steak, rushing to get to the brownie or apple pie that their moms baked for dessert.

I miss fresh food. Mom-food. When we used to eat like that, I thought it was terrible. I wanted pizza pastries and instant everything. But we eat frozen stuff pretty much all the time now: meat-balls and lasagna and weirdly salty single-serving rice and orange chicken. Now the inside of my mouth always tastes like freezer burn and I've forgotten why those dumb dinners ever looked good to begin with.

My stomach churns and growls.

No one is coming, it says. *No one is coming*, it growls. *No one is coming*.

"They are so," I say, maybe out loud, maybe not.

My heart is galloping in my chest like Maximilian, the black horse I used to ride on Saturday mornings back when we had money for that kind of stuff, for real food and for riding lessons and for a house with an actual lawn. I miss Maximilian. I miss my bed and the house and the lawn. I miss everything.

But mostly, I miss not being stuck in a well.

My chest hurts so hard, it makes me sweat. I don't have my inhaler, which is a puff of medicine that opens me up inside like an envelope that you steam open over a kettle on the stove. I can't keep breathing this sharp air! My lungs are gluey. I'm crying now. Again. More and more. I can't not! It's ugly crying, with snot and gagging sounds. I haven't cried like this since Grandma's funeral last July. I think Dad going to jail is what killed her, so if you're wondering why I hate my dad so much, that's reason number one or two or maybe three. All the reasons are big and compete with each other for the top spot.

If I die in this well, I wonder if Dad will be let out of the slammer to come to my funeral. I guess Mandy and Kandy and Sandy will be there, not letting on that it was their fault, dressed in matching black with their hair in some agreed-upon style. I bet they'll weep their little heads right off. I'll bet they'll act like we were best friends. My dad will give them a hug and they'll get to breathe in that smell of him, cigarettes and the Rory Devon cologne that I gave him for Father's Day last year that he insists on wearing even though I hate Rory Devon and his stupid cologne now. (I only liked him for, like, five minutes!) And Juicy Fruit gum. Dad always chews that. I wonder if The Girls will cave then and admit to him that they were the ones who told me to jump onto the well in the first place. I wonder if they'll confess that they laughed when I first fell in. I wonder if they knew the boards were rotten. I wonder if they meant for it to happen.

But mostly, I wonder if my dad will know that it's just one more thing that is all his fault, after all.

4

Luck

My dad went to jail on June 6.

I know that it was June 6 because it was my birthday and that's the kind of detail you don't forget. If it had been any other day, maybe I wouldn't know if it was the 4th or the 5th. But when your dad goes to jail on your birthday, that sticks.

What happened was that Robby and I were lying on the waxy yellow floor of the rec room playing Xbox. We lay on the floor a lot after school that hot June because the floor in there was always cold. The

Xbox was mine—I'd unwrapped it that morning at breakfast—but Robby was already a pro at it and kept telling me what to do. He is always so quick to become an expert. It's the kind of thing that makes me hate him if I think about it too much, the way everything is easy for him and he's just good at it without trying. It's partly because he was 13. I guess stuff gets easier when you're older. There was something wrong with that TV, that's why it was in the basement, in our "playroom" that we called a rec room so we didn't sound like babies. Sometimes the screen would freeze, the pixels all squaring up and then going back to normal in waves, like it wasn't quite sure what it was doing. While we played, we talked or fought but mostly both. Talking to Robby then was like having a really long argument that no one ever won.

Good luck was just one of the billion things that we always debated furiously. Claiming it on my birthday made sense. Birthdays are your power days. They are the days when you get to choose. And it made sense that if one of us got good luck, the other one necessarily wouldn't, so it was important to call it. We battled about it all the time, birthday or not: who saw the first star at night and who won when we pulled wishbones after chicken dinners and whether or not the knife made an unlucky clinking noise when we cut the first piece of birthday cake. The last thing either of us wanted was bad luck, but one of us was always stuck with it, and it was usually me. Robby was a luck hog.

"I call the good luck. It's going to be all mine, I guess," I said airily. "Sorry, unlucky one."

Robby laughed right in my face, up close. His breath stunk like tuna fish. He said that everyone knows that 6-6-6 is the number of the beast, so having my birthday on the sixth day of the sixth month was basically a curse. "Who do you think is gonna be unlucky?" he said. "You were born on Satan Day, basically."

I had this terrible sinking feeling in my stomach because I knew he was right, so I pinched him hard on the arm to get him back, twisting as I pinched. He threw his controller on the floor and he'd just grabbed my arm and pulled it up behind my back in that way that feels like it's about to snap clean in two when Mom opened the door with a bang and said in a really weird voice, "It seems like your father might be in trouble with the law." It sounded like something she'd rehearsed: all stiff and fake, like it was written down and she was being forced at gunpoint to read out loud, like a hostage on CNN.

"What?" I said. "Mom, what?"

Mom didn't answer. She was smoking. The cigarette was dangling there on her Mary Kay coral-lipsticked lips like a fly stuck in flypaper. Mom sold Mary Kay back then. Every morning, she tried a different look, so she knew what she was selling. She doesn't sell it anymore because she doesn't have the time. She says it didn't make enough money to count. But way back then was still Before. When Dad was the smoker, not Mom. Not usually, anyway. I'd hardly ever seen her with a cigarette, even though I knew she sometimes stunk like smoke. The only other time I remembered seeing her smoke was when Grandma had a heart attack and had to go to the hospital to have a stent put in. The cigarette looked weird and wrong, like she'd come into the room wearing Dad's clothes. *Incongruous* is the word, I think. I don't know why I know that word, why I remember that, when I don't remember more important stuff, like (usually) my locker combination.

Then she burst into tears.

"Oh, eff," said Robby, even though we weren't allowed to swear, or even come close to swearing. I gasped. I thought she was going to light into him. I thought she was going to yell at him for sure. But she didn't. She just stood there, staring at us, but like she couldn't even see us. Her eyes didn't blink. I thought about zombies. I was deciding whether or not to be scared.

I looked out the window through the mesh curtains, and saw the flashing red and blue lights on the police car in the driveway. My dad was being led toward it by two policemen who were talking in loud voices, yelling at him. He'd been mowing the lawn in the back, which was a big slope that was great for sledding but stunk for mowing. It was hard work, I guess. His concert T-shirt was soaked with sweat. He had handcuffs on and his shiny bald head was hanging low, like someone guilty on CNN.

"I didn't do it!" he shouted to us as we stood there, gaping, on the front lawn where we had somehow found ourselves. They shoved him into the back of the cruiser like he was a bag of potatoes. Rotten ones. "I didn't do it," he screamed. He was forgetting his right to remain silent, it seemed like.

Even then, I didn't believe him. The sprinklers were on and they sprayed us with water as they twirled around like skaters on the newly cut lawn. Dad always started at the front and mowed it on the diagonal to look like diamond shapes. But none of us moved. We just got wet instead. The car started up and drove away with my dad in the backseat, his face pressed against the window, watching all of us standing there in the rainbow prisms of the water, right there on the perfect patterned grass. Mom's cigarette eventually got so soggy it broke right in half. Then I guess we went in. I don't remember much past that cigarette, dropping down onto the wet green lawn.

I haven't seen Dad since. Mom saw him a lot during the trial, but she said we couldn't go because kids weren't allowed. She said he looked "fine." She said he was sooooo sorry he'd done it. She said that if he had to go to prison, he knew he deserved it and when he got out, everything would be OK again. She said he'd make it up to us.

I didn't believe that. I still don't. You can't ever believe liars. They lie.

The trial went on for a long time. Eventually, Mom stopped talking to us about it at all. She tried so hard to make it "normal" that it was anything but. Like who cared what happened at school at lunch time? What difference did it make what I got on my times tables quiz? I asked her stuff about court and Dad and she asked me stuff about school, and neither of us answered anything and I stood in her room and ironed her clothes for her while she sat on the edge of the bed and rubbed her feet. I don't know why her feet hurt so much. It was like all the pain in her heart had just sunk down her legs and got stuck there.

I liked ironing. I especially loved the smell of hot clothes but not so much when they weren't clean, when the iron brought out the burnt cigarette stink of them. It was hard to know if I should mention how terrible it was that she suddenly loved to smoke those disgusting cigarettes. Everyone knows it kills you! Why would you start something that you know is terrible? Who does that? That's when I got scared. That's when I got mad.

After I ironed, I'd lie down next to her on the bed and turn on the TV. I'd pretend I didn't hate her.

Hating both your parents is really exhausting, but it's not like I had a choice.

When Dad was sentenced, it was all over the news and the Internet. People went crazy for the story because it was so terrible. What he did, I mean. People gobbled it up, cackling, like they couldn't believe anyone would do anything so purely vile. The picture they used was one from his job, the one that was on his ID badge. It made him look sneaky and smug, like someone who had been caught with his hand in the cookie jar (which I guess he was), but who had gotten away with it (which he didn't). I think someone photoshopped what was left of his hair to make it look the tiniest bit like devil horns. I wondered if, even while he grinned for the picture, he was planning to do what he did. I'll never ask him, so I guess I'll never know.

Marianne Singleton read that stupid article, the one basically everyone read, out loud in her high, clear voice in the afternoon during Current Events class. That was a class we had where you had to Google something interesting and then print out what you found and share it with everyone, if by "share it," I mean "read it out loud." I hate reading out loud. I am the tiniest bit dyslexic. Sometimes words trip my tongue. Marianne wasn't dyslexic, not even a little. Worse, she had details I hadn't found out yet.

I hadn't been on the computer. Mom had told me not to, and seriously, I just didn't want to know. That morning, she'd handed me a printed-out story about someone robbing a bank up in Canada somewhere and escaping with a team of sled dogs. "For Current Events," she said. "I thought you'd like this one." I used to *love* sled dogs. Any kind of dog, but especially the ones with the ice-blue eyes. I'd felt happy and special, like she'd been thinking of me, taking care of me, even if she was slowly killing herself at the same time. I guess she'd been protecting me so that I didn't see my dad, grinning guiltily out at me from my home page. *His* ice-blue eyes, I could live without.

Before Marianne started to read, she shot me a sympathetic smile, which I could tell she thought was really nice. It looked fake. Then she cleared her throat and went for it. I couldn't believe that Mr. Johnson let her read it! That he didn't jump out of his orange chair and shout, "STOP!" He just listened. He just watched. When she was finished reading, there was a terrible, awkward silence and then, just like that, everyone in fifth grade at Huntington Elementary swiveled their heads around on their necks like a whole parliament of owls to stare at me, suddenly stuffed full of the knowledge that my dad was guilty of embezzling and was going to prison for six years.

Of course, then I had to hate them, too. For knowing. For staring. For all of it.

I sat there at my desk and did the math on a piece of scrap paper where I'd written half of a "Hi!" note to my best friend, Tracy, who had been ignoring me since the trial started, but who I was hoping to win back with smileys and nice notes. I'd gotten as far as "Hi!" and then had run out of things to say. So I crossed it out and wrote $11 + 6 = 17$. I could have done it in my head, but I didn't want to. Writing it down made me feel busy. I would be 17 when he got out! I would be a completely different person. He was going to miss everything! My heart broke in two like a cereal bowl that's been dropped off the counter, splashing milk and corn-flakes everywhere, much like mine had this morning. (I should have known it was going to basically be the worst day of my life, so far.)

I scribbled out the equation with my pencil so

that soon it was just a charcoal-gray blur. Then I put my head down on my desk. I covered the back of my head with my hands, like we were on an airplane and it was about to crash. I pretended to be invisible. I almost believed I was until I opened my eyes and saw that everyone was still staring at me.

Then the kids started putting up their hands and asking questions. Mr. Johnson asked if I wanted to leave the room and I shook my head, my forehead pressed down on the paper, because no, and because I couldn't stand up anyway because my knees were shaking too bad to use as supportive-limbs-that-hold-up-a-body. He talked about how my dad had taken all this money from his work and put it into his own bank account instead. Was that wrong, boys and girls? Yes, it was. *Duh*. He talked about how my dad was going to prison and how he would eat all his food there and sometimes play basketball for recreation. My dad hated basketball. He was terrible at it. I groaned.

To be honest, up until then, I didn't really know that *embezzling* meant stealing money. I thought it was something to do with hair. The word sounds like fuzz escaping from braids that you've slept in. All at once, my forehead pressed so hard against my desktop that it was getting bruised, I understood how we had money for riding lessons and a big house and a really nice SUV and more than one plasma TV, when Alice's dad had the same job as Dad and they had to live in an apartment and take the bus because they couldn't afford a car. Up until that moment, I had just assumed Alice's dad was really bad at his job, sort of like how Alice is terrible at gymnastics, baseball, and everything else. I had thought my dad was just a superstar. I guess I thought I was, too. I could do a cartwheel and roundoffs and smash a baseball into left field without even really trying.

When I got home from school, a purplish bruise marked my forehead like an ugly tattoo, right next to the shiny gray splotch that I got from putting my head on my scribbles. I hid it with my bangs, not that anyone was asking, but because I guess I wanted to hide it from myself.

The bruises that I have now, I couldn't hide from anyone, especially not from me. I don't know what I look like, but everywhere that my body is pressed up against this stupid dusty brick hurts, exactly like my forehead hurt that day when I pressed it with my finger. I close my eyes and imagine my arms and legs purpling up, black and green and yellow and all the rainbow colors that my forehead was, like ink slipping around under my skin.

It's not fair, that's all I can think. *It's not fair, it's not fair, it's not fair.* "Life isn't fair," Grandma used to say. And she's right, it's not, *especially* when you are stuck in a well, purpling up like a grape juice spill on a white carpet. My old room had white carpet. My old room had a grape juice spill that looked just like Australia that I hid under a potted plant beside my desk.

Not long after Dad went to jail, the bank took our house and all the stuff in it, including that stained old white carpet, and we moved to Hell, which is in Texas. The town isn't really called Hell, but that's what Robby calls it and I don't think

he's wrong. It's not even really a town. I call it Nowheresville. It's sort of like a patch of scrubland
with a couple of big warehouses plonked down on
it that store stuff that people buy on the Internet.
There is also a brewery. Everyone's parents basically work in the warehouse or at the brewery. Mom
works at both.

The town stinks all the time, not as badly as this
well, but pretty bad. Making beer is not a process
that makes good smells. Robby calls the stink "beer
farts." That's about what it smells like. It's terrible.

But the worst thing about Nowheresville is that
there is no skating rink. Skating was my favorite
sport. I was going to compete this year. I had a rou-
tine and everything. I was ready. But I guess it's
just too bad for me. Anyway, now my skates are
too small and I can't afford new ones and maybe
leaving New Jersey and ice skating and horseback
riding and things that I was good at behind is what
happens when your dad is the bad guy. No more
sit spins for me. No more axels or toe loops or sal-
chows. That's fine, I guess. It just wasn't meant to

be. I'm OK with it. Some dreams are dumb, anyway. Not everyone can win Olympic gold medals. Not everyone can be the very best at everything they ever do. Probably pretty soon, I would have gotten bad at skating. Eventually other kids would have been better and I would have quit. So it's fine that it happened this way. Really.

The main street in Nowheresville has "everything we need" according to Mom, which means there is a supermarket and a library and a bank and a really gross diner and a gas station and a Dunkin' Donuts. The record store is the best thing in the whole town. It's the coolest. Dad would love it, because the owner also likes old vinyl records. It's like there are two types of people in the world who love vinyl: guys like my dad who just like to own stuff, and hipsters like Record Store Dave who for real believe the music sounds better that way.

It makes me happy that we have this great record store and Dad can't shop there, which is mean, but I can't help it. He doesn't deserve to. The store sells regular CDs and stuff, too. Plus random things, like bobbleheads of pop stars and old concert posters. It has speakers outside that pour music onto the sidewalk, thick as a milkshake, filling up the air with all those bubbles of sound. There are chairs where you can sit and just listen, which I've done five or six times now, pretending that I'm not nervous to do it, pretending that I don't look as small as a six-year-old in those big chairs. Sometimes I like sitting there, and sometimes I don't. Mostly I do.

Record Store Dave sometimes comes out and sits next to me, sort of like Mr. Thacker, but he doesn't make me talk. He's kind of great. I like him. If I could make any wish in the world come true, I would wish for my mom to go in there one day and to fall in love with Record Store Dave. I want her to marry Dave. I want Dave to be my dad because Record Store Dave is every bit of the man that Dad is not. He's honest, for one. I want him to fill up our ugly trailer with his music that he actually listens to instead of just collecting it in boxes so he can say,

"Yeah, I own one of only ten copies of that super-famous Beatles record whatever whatever." What's the point of music you don't listen to?

Dave always smiles like nothing could ever be wrong. I'd never say that out loud. I'm only mentioning it now because I'm in a well and I might probably die—of starvation, if nothing else—so why not? If this is a wishing well, I can make a wish on myself. I can be the lucky penny. If I was going to make two more wishes, I would wish to be out of this well, obviously, and I would also wish for a cheeseburger with a side of fries and a huge chocolate shake made from real ice cream. I am so hungry I could practically eat the dead thing that's below me, but, actually, no. I'm not *that* hungry. Now I feel sick and hungry at the same time, which is a pretty terrible combination.

We ate at the diner once and I was sick for a week. I had meatloaf and macaroni because Mom used to make that stuff and even if I hated it then, I missed it now. That dinner came out both ends for days. It wasn't even good going in, so you can imagine what that week was like. Afterward, I felt like my legs were made of elastic bands.

Up until Dad did what he did, I don't remember ever feeling like my legs were going to let me down. They'd always done everything I'd ever asked of them, pushing me off the ice and twirling me around on it and all of that. I guess that my strength is just one more thing Dad took, along with all that money.

The school is partway out of town on the highway and we have to walk to it, whether or not our legs are too weak for the job. It's not like the town was really planned; the warehouses were just built there because the land was cheap, and the town came up next to them so the workers would have a place to live. I'd ride my bike to school, but we don't have bikes anymore, and we're too close for the bus, and besides, I hate school buses with the heat of a thousand Texas suns. Everything bad that goes on at school goes on with a thousand times more intensity on a school bus. Trust me.

Mom had to sell the car when we got here so we

could pay rent on our new house, which isn't even a house, it's a trailer. I try to pretend that we're camping, like it's practically a camper, and everyone knows that campers are fun. We went camping the summer before Dad got caught. We rented a motor home that had a bunk above the driver's seat. That was fun. It was the best. I'm good at pretending, but not that good. No one would *camp* in this ugly trailer park. It's too gross. There's nowhere to go swimming or anything fun to do. Everyone smokes and has dogs and shouts a lot inside their trailer walls. At night, I lie awake and listen to glass breaking and too-loud laughter and trying-to-be-quiet crying. In the morning, I'm always surprised that the ground isn't covered with shards of glass, ankle deep, surrounding us like a dangerous flood that has risen overnight, slicing perfect letter J's into our bare toes.

Robby and I have to share a room now. Not much could be worse than that. He'll maybe be happy when I die in this well and he gets that ugly orange room all to himself. The place came furnished and even the curtains are orange. The carpet, the bed-spreads that smell like some other kids' farts, the paint on the walls. I don't know for sure, but I'm pretty certain that orange is the official color of despair.

And carrots.

The Girls have been gone for a long time. I'm trying not to think the worst, which makes me think the worst. Mr. Thacker and I talked a lot about how trying not to think of a thing makes you think of a thing. Well, I am definitely not trying to think about how I AM GOING TO DIE HERE ALONE AND THEY AREN'T COMING BACK.

I start to cry again. In case you thought I was crying that whole time, I should say that I stopped for a while and now I've started up again. No one can hear me, but I don't care, I can't really help it. Crying because you're sad is unstoppable; it just happens, even if you close your eyes, it leaks out of you. Sadness makes you holey, like a sieve, and nothing can be held in. I'm sad that I'm going to die. I'm mourning myself.

I wonder what I would have been when I grew up if I'd lived. I bet I would have had a smart job, like a scientist or someone who reads the news on TV. I bet I could have been in the Olympics after all, skating or horseback riding or even both. I'd definitely have won a few Oscars for being a movie star, or at least an MTV award. I might have even been President. I mean, why not? It's about time there was a girl in that job. Women are just as good as men. Everyone knows *that*, it's just that some men are scared of that truth so they claw their way to the top and push women down whenever they can, keeping the top spot for themselves.

Jerks.

I wonder where The Girls ran to and who they are getting to come and help. The police? The firemen? The dads are all still at work, I guess, although I don't know what time it is—my stomach and the fading blue of the sky make me think it's definitely after four, maybe even five—but it doesn't matter, because everyone works shifts and no one's dads ever seem to be home.

The closest house is Amanda's. Her mom doesn't have a job, she's the only mom who doesn't. She vacuums all day. Their carpet is purest white—not a grape juice stain in sight—with this soft, long pile, so that where she's vacuumed, it leaves a pattern like a freshly mown lawn.

I miss having a lawn. When we had a lawn, we would run through Dad's automated sprinkler system, jumping on the sprinkler heads and sometimes accidentally breaking them so that the water sprayed out every which way but the right way. Afterwards, when we were shivering from all that water, we'd eat popsicles that were so cold they stuck to our tongues. Only then would we lie in the sun to warm back up, slathered in suntan lotion to block out everything about the sun except the heat, of course. No one wants cancer. I mean, duh. Although here in Hell, no one seems to care like they did at home. Here, a lot of people smoke. Here, wearing sunscreen isn't really a thing.

That dumb sprinkler makes me think of Dad driving away in that patrol car, nose pressed to the glass, his breath fogging it up. "Nostalgia is a terrible thing," Grandma used to say, and I think I finally get what she means. She means that remembering stuff stinks. It's maybe even the worst. Not as bad as dying in a well, but close.

The fading sky is now pretty undeniably unblue. It's definitely the dull gray of past dinnertime and now I'm sure The Girls aren't coming back. Someone's mom or dad had to have been home by now. At least one of them. Kandy's dad is a supervisor, he works normal-ish hours. He's always home by dinner, at least.

I'm crying super softly now because I really don't want to trigger an asthma attack. I've only ever had one, once, and that's when I found out that I'm allergic to goats. But you never know. Maybe the dead thing down there is a goat. Maybe a whole herd of goats trampled onto the entrance to this well and fell down, one by one, and then one day someone just threw a board over the top because they were tired of losing their goats. Maybe this is going to be the ironic thing, after all, that goats will be what kill me in the end.

I wish I wasn't dizzy.

I wish I could breathe.

I wish those girls would come back and hurry and hurry and hurry.

5

AdRIft

I'm drifting and fading. I've come loose from myself
and I'm floating down instead of up, a slow sinking,
a darkness falling. I don't think I'm scared now,
but maybe I am. No one is coming. I keep saying
it to myself: *No one is coming.* But I can't hear me.
Something is sniffing and scuffling. I look up and
see the darkening sky through my round window
on the world. The branch moves back and forth,
and back and forth.

Snuffle, scuffle, sniff. I hope it isn't a coyote, but

even if it is, it can't get to me in the well, unless maybe it falls down too. I guess the silver lining to that would be that I wouldn't be alone anymore. Maybe the coyote is silver. Maybe silver coyotes eat goats. I'm almost sure they do. Silver linings are everywhere. Maybe this whole well is lined with silver. Maybe if I shined a light at the walls, they'd shimmer like tinfoil. I'm the potato, wrapped in the foil, about to get tossed on the campfire. Except there's no fire and I'm so cold and silver is my least favorite metal. I like gold better, and bronze even better than that. *That's just like you*, Robby would say, *to like the color that means third place. You're such a loser, Loser.*

You're a loser, I'd say back. *You're Prince Loser of Losertown, Lord of Losertania.*

And he'd be like, *That isn't even funny, it's just dumb, Dumbo. Queen Dumbo of Dumboland.*

Robby would be able to use his boy-strength to get out of this well without a rope. That's the kind of thing he does. He gets out of trouble. I fall into wells. When I finally get out, he'll probably say, "Why'd you stay down there so long? Are you retarded?"

And I'll say, "Don't use that word, you freak."

And he'll say, "Don't call me a freak, you jerk."

And then I'll probably punch him or maybe do that thing where I push in the back of his knees and he falls over. And then he'll probably punch me back or sit on me and spit onto my face, that long gob of saliva dangling over my lips. And then I'll probably throw up.

I miss Robby and all his gangly strength and the way he hops up and down from foot to foot when he's waiting for something to happen, like he has too much energy to actually contain in his human body.

"Help," I say, just to see if my voice still works or to see if the silent silver has stolen my sounds away. I sound croaky, like a frog. A hopping frog. Robby, the jumping frog. Dad used to say Robby was frogging when he hopped from foot to foot. "Stop frogging, Robb-o," he'd say. "You're making me tired." And Robby would stop frogging. Dad had that kind of power. I'd say, "Stop frogging, Robb-o," and he'd say, "Zip it, Skippy," and he'd frog even more. Frog, frog, frog. *Ribbit, ribbit.*

"Woe is me," I croak to the imaginary silver coyote that's fallen on my head. Then in a French accent, "Vat did ve do to deserve this, *mon ami? Zut alors! Au secours!*"

No one in Nowheresville speaks French, except for *le coyote d'argent*, naturally. Animals know either all languages or none, I forget which. I learned French the summer before last at camp. It was French or canoeing, and I don't like the water any more than I like the fish that lurk around in it, looking hungrily at all that skin on your bare, kicking legs.

"*Je ne sais pas,*" my imaginary head-coyote says. "*Je t'aime. Ou est la salle de bain?*"

Then we're quiet for a while because that is all the French I know, and I guess it's the limit of his vocabulary, too. Maybe if I knew the real French word for coyote, we'd be better friends and he'd save me, knitting me a rope ladder to the top out of his silky fur.

"*Au revoir*," I say to him, and then he's gone in a shivery blink.

I hear more footsteps.

"Croak, croak," I croak and the animal barks, *Le woof! Le woof!* He is also *français*! *Mon dieu!* Maybe it is Lassie, this time! Lassie is a dog from an old TV show. Robby and I, we watched all of those shows. After a while, they were boring, but there was something good about them, too. They were like the hand-knitted afghans that you cover yourself with at your Grandma's house. Boring, safe, slightly annoying. Lassie was a bit like that, but she also always saved the day. No one was ever left to die. Not in one single episode.

"Lassie!" I shout. "I am in the well! I mean, *Je suis* in the well! *Dans* the well! *Dans LE* well!"

We never used to watch dumb old shows like *Lassie* back in New Jersey. We watched reality TV, like *The Singer* with Mom and Dad on the massive TV in the living room, which is one of the many things that is now gone gone gone into a huge underground storage tank at the bank where they keep the things stolen by wrongdoers. The TV. The living room. Our life. I picture it all down there, set up just how it was, maybe with Monopoly out on the table and me and Robby frozen in place, wrestling over who gets to be the racecar. Mom used to think game nights were "healthy." We were the only kids I knew who actually played board games with their parents once a week. I liked it. I'd never tell anyone that, though. I'd just roll my eyes and pretend it was dumb. It wasn't dumb. It was the best.

Back in the day, me and Robby would lie on the carpet and *The Singer* would come on and Mom and Dad got the couch because that's just how it was: kids on the floor, parents on the furniture. Sometimes I'd put my face so close to the TV that Dad said that I'd go blind and then we'd all laugh and hoot and howl because not one kid ever in history went blind from sitting too close to the TV and besides, it was plasma. We were a family of laughers. We liked to laugh. I'd be interested to meet that kid, if it ever happened that their fancy TV blinded him. Maybe his seeing-eye dog would look like Lassie.

Parents are programmed like robots to say "Don't sit so close!" and "No talking back!" since the old days when maybe you *could* have gone blind from sitting too close to the TV. When you don't want to eat your disgusting kale-and-tofu "scramble," they automatically say, "There are starving children in Africa!" as if you can just either eat the sludge or get yourself to Africa and start sharing like a kindergartener who is trying to earn a gold star sticker.

It occurs to me right at this exact moment that it's possible children could be raised by robots *better* than by actual people because robot dads are unlikely to go to prison for embezzling. And then robot moms would not have to take on more than one job stuffing boxes full of all the future garbage that people who haven't gone to jail yet for stealing buy on the Internet with a *click-click* of their mouse, their credit cards burning up from all that spending.

"It's difficult," Mom says, "when you see what people buy. It's so *much*, that's all." I know what she means. But then again, Dad used to do that, too. So it's hard to fault them, all these faceless strangers with the toys and socks they buy on the Internet, along with diapers and a new watch and the whole series of *My Family of Giants* on DVD.

Back then, when we used to watch *My Family of Giants*, Mom would say, "Your head makes a better door than a window!" which both Mom and Dad thought was hilarious and they'd fall onto the sofa laughing. And Dad would choke out, "If you're a window, open the blinds!" and they would literally scream with laughter.

OK, that only happened once. But I could see it happening again and again, if nothing had changed. Mom and Dad were the kind of people who liked to really get their money's worth out of a joke. Or, I guess, Dad would steal the money to buy the joke and then the bank would reclaim it. *Ba-dum cha.* *That* was a joke. I'm trying to find it reassuring that, even though I'm in a well and my entire body hurts and is possibly purple, I can still find humor in things. Laughter is the best medicine! That's another Grandma-ism. Sadly, it is not enough medicine to help me actually feel any less scared, or any less hurt.

I close my eyes for a second, like that might help me forget where I am, but I have to open them again really fast because closing them makes me feel like I'm spinning. Feeling like you are spinning while also being pinned in place in a well is very disconcerting. I curl my tongue and take a breath in through it, like it's a straw. That's a yoga thing that Mom once tried to teach me, back when she used to do yoga because she had time for stuff like that. You're also supposed to swallow your breath, but I try that, and it hurts really bad all the way down, and then I get the hiccups. It really doesn't get much better than this—hiccupping, bruised, bleeding, and trapped. Seriously, this is pushing the limits of how life isn't fair into a whole other thing. I don't know what I mean by that. My head feels strange.

Anyway, Lassie was always saving people from wells back when dogs did that sort of thing. If you think about it, it couldn't happen now because everyone's dog is on a chain or locked up in a yard. If they run free, then everyone starts a petition about vicious dogs, and the dog is picked up by the dog catcher and accidentally put to sleep in a "shelter," leaving the family to weep their bitter tears all over their faces. That happened once last year when Mark Fleetman's dog escaped from his electric fence. The dog was a pit bull named Macy. She was the sweetest, nicest dog ever, but I guess the dog catcher didn't agree, because one day she was there and the next—gone.

Of course, now that I'm actually *in* a well, I know that *Lassie* was not a very realistic show, because when they pulled the kid out of the well on *Lassie*, the kid was just dirty, not all scraped up and bloody and croaking like an asthmatic frog who smokes and is allergic to dead goats. TV is another thing that is all a lie. For example, Kandy, Mandy, and Sandy can't seriously believe that they will one day win one of the following two shows: *The Singer* or *Fashion's Best Face*. Ha freaking *ha*. That's just plain dumb! When you take those girls out of No-wheresville, Texas, they're just ordinary. They are only special here because there aren't very many people. It's not hard to climb to the top of a pile of 50 kids if you've got the money to buy the best clothes and stuff. It's a lot harder to scale a heap of, say, a million. Or more.

The number of people who believe the World's Biggest Lie is depressingly huge. It's like, all of them. Everyone believes that you can do anything you want to do. You can be anyone you want to be. Seriously. WRONG. The number of people who have figured it out is one. And that one person is me. But I'm going to take all that knowledge with me when I die in this well. That's not even ironic, it's just too bad for me and for all of mankind. One day all those people are going to be mightily disappointed. And by "all those people," I mean Mandy, Kandy, and Sandy. And secretly, I'm glad.

I hope they grow up to be sorry.

I sigh hard and choke on the silver dust and Lassie does not come for me and no one barks in any language and I'm alone in a well and I'm going to die. Well. Well, well, well, I'm in a well.

Something is crawling on my foot.

I scream, scream, scream, because of the something that is crawling on my foot. The screaming makes me cough and splutter, silver spraying everywhere around me in a shower of metallic rainbows. A spider! A spider! I can't see it, but it's *probably* a spider. Or a crab. How would a crab get into a well? Of course it's a spider! Not a crab. There aren't crabs in wells. Or in Texas at all, as far as I can tell. Not this part of it anyway. Maybe at the shore. I've never been to a Texan beach, but I guess there's such a thing, there must be. We live in the dry part where there are snakes withering inside their see-through skins, and truck-driving men with mustaches and plaid shirts, and girls with fancy clothes who think it's OK to trick you into falling down a well, and spiders with pointy crab feet, scuttling. Here, even the sky is thirsty, and now it's a wanting kind of flat gray, like it's yearning for blackness to fill it up, to saturate it.

Texas ain't all it's cracked up to be, Grandma would say. You'd think she talked a lot more than she really did. She was actually a quiet person. Maybe that's the secret: to not say very much, but to make sure everything you do say is quotable later by people who have fallen down old wells.

It doesn't get worse than being a Grandma-quoting well-bound girl in Texas with a crabby spider on your foot, unless you're in a well full of water and fish. Fish are worse. That's comforting, except not really. I try to flick my foot against the wall to knock the spider crab off, but then I can't tell if it is gone or not, or if it has bitten me or not, or if, after all, it's just that my foot is asleep due to the circulation having been cut off to my poor old blackened and bleeding legs. But let's not overlook the terrifying possibilities, OK? Maybe it is a black widow!

I start to sweat. Sweating is one of the symptoms of black widow bites, so clearly I am not only right, I am also dying. We watched a terrible video about spiders last year at school. It was all about seeping skin and black laughing arachnids. Actually, now that I think about it, sweating might have been a symptom of a different spider bite. I think black widows paralyze you so you can't breathe.

Coincidentally, I can't breathe.

"I don't want to die!" I say out loud, like the well can hear me and will save me, maybe by spitting me out in a shimmering shower of lights, like dancers bursting out onto a stage during a Rory Devon concert, fireworks included, the fireworks of me.

The well is an animal that's holding me in its throat, thinking about swallowing me down all the way. I pat its wall. "Please don't hurt me," I say. "I won't hurt you." Maybe the well is just misunderstood like sasquatches and monsters always are in books. Or maybe there is no air down here and my brain is just mashing up a bunch of crazy lies and making them seem real and true, like grapes turning to wine under the bare feet of some hairy Greek men. There actually isn't any air down here. The goats took it all. Goats are greedy and take take

take. My dad is a goat. I'm thirsty like a dried-out snake. Maybe this isn't an air problem, but a water problem. Who says there is a problem?

My foot is itchy now but I can't reach it, and that's when I realize that my shoe must have fallen off because it's definitely not on my foot, protecting it from snakes and dead goat zombies and rampaging, well-dwelling spiders and crabs. Everyone knows that socks are useless as armor. They are soft and flop at the first sign of danger. I can't even tell if they are still on me, but the shoe is definitely gone. They were new shoes! I used all of the money that I had left in my bank account to buy them. I wore my regular old shoes to school on my first day at Nowheresville Middle School and a boy named Brendan Wilson said that they looked like shoes I had stolen from a bum. Actually, what he said was, "What hobo did you rumble to grab those lame sneaks?" I feel like I need a decoder ring to understand what Brendan Wilson is saying. Luckily, he rarely talks to me.

"They're just dirty!" I said.

"Ha," he said. "Gruesome twosome."

"Whatever that means," I said, being the new tough-cool-version of myself.

"Did your mom steal them from the warehouse?" he said.

"No," I said, and punched him in the stomach. He bent in half like grass in the wind and walked away, all bent over. I don't know why I did that. I don't know why he didn't tell. I don't know why I didn't think to get Mom to order those stupid shoes from the warehouse's website. They probably would've been half the price.

I could have even just put the old shoes in the washing machine at the Laundromat. They have one of those big ones that you could put anything in: shoes, blankets, your brother. (I wish.) But I really wanted the shoes that I'd seen in the window of the big department store in the next town over, where you can buy vacuum cleaners and coats and bicycles and iPhones and, yes, sneakers. Everything and anything is available there, which is super dumb now that I think of it, because probably everyone shops at the warehouse's site. Why wouldn't they? They probably get a discount! That store is not long for this world.

Anyway, I took all the money I had left in the world and I went and bought them. The store is old-fashioned. The lady at the cash register was about a hundred years old and called me Sweetheart. The shoes are Adidas, which are the best and coolest. They are white with three of the palest blue stripes on the side. They're the nicest things I've bought since Dad's downfall. And now one of them is at the bottom of the well and/or in China and/or has been eaten by an undead goat.

I start to cry again, but my throat is all clamped up from all that crying before and I can't breathe, so I stop and instead do useful things, like whisper-screaming *HELP* every twelve seconds in the hopes of being helped.

Twelve is my lucky number. When I'm 12, I think I'll probably have a really good year and get all the luck. If you think about it, turning 12 on the sixth day of the sixth month has to be lucky because 6 and 6 are 12, but twelving them eradicates their six-iness, removing the bad-luck beast. I'll probably run away when I'm 12 and start over, get a whole new life without an annoying older brother and an exhausted, overworked mother and a dad who is rotting away in prison.

Or I'll be dead.

In a well.

With some goats.

I guess you just never know with this life. You never quite know what is coming next.

6

Cats

I did not mention before about how my mother is crazy, but that doesn't make it less of a fact. Since Dad went to jail, she has gone totally bonkers, insane-o-rama, around the bend. Other than working, which she does all the time, and smoking, which is her new and completely crazy and expensive and dumb habit, the other thing my mother now does is collect cats. Right before I left the trailer park to meet The Girls to do their club initiation (i.e., getting my hair massacred and falling into a well), Mr.

Sutton, who owns our place, knocked on the door and gruffly handed me a notice to give to my Mom when she got home from her job at the brewery, which is where she is today, stirring a bubbling vat of hops that will make her stink for days and days. She calls them "hopes" instead of hops. "Just stirring the hopes today," she'll say. "Maybe I'll throw in some dreams." Some of the time Mom makes more sense than others.

Mr. Sutton has a long mustache and a plaid shirt, like everyone else in town who is a man. He is trying to grow a beard, but the wisps of hair on his chin make me think of newborn babies. I feel bad for him. No one wants a baby-head on their manly chin. The hair on his chest is worse though. That stuff makes it look like he is permanently hugging a baby chimp which is showing through the gaps in his pearly buttons. In other words, he's the grossest, most disgusting, pathetic excuse for a human being, ever. I'm pretty sure he chose the orange décor in this dump. He likes orange. His hair is orange. His skin is also a little orange, but that may just be the fake tanner he uses because he for real gets terrible sunburns in the actual sun. Living in Texas was his first mistake. Ours too, come to think of it. I thanked him for the letter as sweetly as I could. I just felt like if he thought I was sweet he'd have mercy on us. I should have known better.

As soon as he left, I steamed open his letter and read it. Who writes letters in this day and age? He should have just texted her but—actually—no, she doesn't have a cell phone anymore, so forget that. Well, he could have called. Mr. Sutton must have known that we're too poor for technology. Where is his sympathy? Where is his kindness?

The letter was written in capital letters on yellow lined paper. It said that Mom's cats were a health hazard, and either they had to go or we would be evicted. I glued the envelope shut again with a glue stick and left it on the table where she'd see it. I hope I put the glue away. If I didn't, then she'll know what I did and then I'll be in for it for reading her mail and for trying to pretend that I didn't. Or what if I left the kettle on? Maybe the whole place will burn down. Silver lining: It will take the evidence of my crime with it.

But it would also burn up all of the cats. The cats! Well, I hate the cats, but I hope they don't die or anything. That would be terrible, too. I don't hate *all* cats, so scrap that thought. I'm scared of (most) cats. Have you ever looked at their eyes? Slits! Strange slitty eyes! That follow you! One of the cats, Cat, is always following me around. He watches everything I do. I feel like Cat is taking notes. When I try to get into Heaven (which may be sooner than planned), Cat will probably provide God with a list of reasons why I'm actually a terrible person. The rest of the cats are better than Cat, but not by much. I mean, it's not like he sets the bar particularly high.

The fact is, the cats smell bad and only love you when you have cat food in your hand. Mom has somehow managed to accumulate 11 cats so far. I don't know how it happens! She goes to the store for milk or cigarettes, and comes back with four frozen dinners and a kitten. She comes home from work, and dumps a kitten out of her purse. She goes out on the crooked front steps and has a cigarette, and comes back in with a kitten in her hands. She's like a cat goddess with no actual powers except drawing cats to her and then having to take care of them and clean out their litter. Lucky for her, they mostly don't use it, so that is not the worst part of cleaning up after the cats.

We stopped naming them after the first eight, which is why we have Happy, Dopey, Sleepy, Sneezy, Grumpy, Doc, Bashful, Rory Devon and then just three random orange ones that we call "Cat." I can't tell if all three of them follow me or if it's just one. They are identical triplets. The threeing of Cat is probably what makes him/her particularly evil.

I named Rory Devon to bug Robby. Everyone tells Robby that he looks like Rory Devon, which he does, but also everyone hates The Devs, including him. (Except for me. I'm probably going to marry him one day, so I am careful to only hate him enough to fit in, while still secretly knowing that we are connected by true love.) When someone tells Robby that he's looking a little Rory-y, you can see his fists clenching by his sides. The thing is, if he wanted to look less like Rory Devon, he could stop combing his hair in that particular way. (It looks good on Rory, but not so much on Robby.)

Rory Devon (the cat) is missing all of his teeth and spends a lot of time yowling. If you generously think of the yowling as singing, you can appreciate how he's living up to his name, or trying to. If any cat is going to rescue me from the well, it will probably be Rory Devon. He seems like a cat who is just waiting for his heroic nature to shine through, to compensate for his terrible vocals and gaping tooth sockets. He's also practically a dog in his mannerisms and fondness for belly rubs. He's actually a bit of a special cat. I almost feel like me and The Devs are on the same wavelength. For example, sometimes when I feel lonely or sad, I think really hard about that cat and he always appears. It would be so fantastic if he suddenly appeared now. I close my eyes and think very hard about his frowny little cat face. I try to will him to come to me, to save me.

It's important to be optimistic, even when everything is terrible, that's what I think. Grandma always said that my spunkiness was unparalleled. If she could see me now, still trying to be spunky while I'm trapped in a well, she'd be so proud. She was proud of me once before when I won the kids' baking category at the county fair when I was 6. She actually baked the cookies, so that was cheating, and now that I think about it, she was obviously just proud of herself.

In fact, she was just another liar.

She always said she was The Matriarch, which means the powerful woman who is basically the boss of the family. Well, that may be true. She was certainly The Matriarch of the Lying Family of Liars. I guess it's likely that I am a liar too, genetically speaking, and just don't know it. Maybe I lie to myself about lying, like any liar would. I blame Grandma. Now it's in our blood, the same way that none of us can see anything but a swirling blur of colors without glasses on, and we all hate beets and being up too high on ladders. And clowns. We all hate clowns. Clowns are the worst of all our fears. I'm picturing clowns laughing at me in the well. I can practically see them, miming and gesturing with their red noses and fake tears and plastic hair and now I want to scream. THANKS A LOT, GRANDMA, FOR MAKING ME THINK OF CLOWNS WHILE I'M IN A WELL.

Oh, *Grandma*. Why are you dead? You would know how to save me. I don't know how, exactly, but you'd figure it out. Some people are just people who solve problems. Grandma was one of them. One time, Robby and I got stuck up at the top of the apple tree in her backyard and couldn't get down. I had gone up first, and he had come up to save me when I got stuck. She marched into the garage, found the extension ladder, and extended it, climbed up, and fetched us. Now that I think of it, of course a ladder is an obvious solution to getting kids down from trees and anyone would have thought of that. Still, there are probably other examples.

It was cancer. Cancer won against Grandma. Obituaries in the paper always say things like,

"After a valiant fight!" which makes me think of knights, battling to the death with swords. Cancer is a very good swordsman, I guess. Grandma was only 63 and she wasn't ruthless or any of the other things you need to be to win a duel with cancer.

I wonder if being dead and buried is really that much different from being in a well. I guess the major difference is that I can see light (what's left of it, anyway) and she can't. Unless she's in Heaven, if it exists, in which case she is basking in a lovely warm glow and I'm the only one who is stuck in the cold darkness, unable to get into Heaven. Unfair. Not that Grandma deserves to be trapped in a well, but I guess I'd rather she was in a well than dead. The well wouldn't have been so final. Maybe she could have won against the well. But if she's going to be dead and buried anyway, I'm sorry to say that I'd rather it was her down here than me.

I shiver because it's starting to get chilly and I don't have a jacket and I'm in a freezing cold well. Also, thinking about death makes me cold, and possibly the poison from the spider bite that is slowly killing me has a chilling effect.

"Rory Devon!" I yell. "Lassie!"

There is no answer. Duh. It's as quiet as being in a pool with your ears full of water. I like pools. That might surprise you as I mostly hate water things, but pools don't have fish, so they are safe. Plus, they always smell like clean chemicals and lifeguards.

The wind has dropped off and the branch has stopped waving back and forth and back and forth. I miss it. Maybe that branch was Grandma, signaling to me from the other side! Maybe she was saying, "I'm sorry I lied about the cookies!" I hope so. I miss Grandma, that crazy old liar.

I hold my breath so that I can hear Rory Devon when he comes to save me. The trouble with cats is that they aren't dogs. They can't sense when you've fallen down a well! They don't bother themselves with saving you either, evidently. Stupid cats. Right now, Rory Devon is probably stretching in the patch of sunlight that streams across my pillow in the late afternoon, warm and comfortable, tuning out my cries for help. Down with cats!

Mom must be home from work by now. I wonder if she'll read that letter and then sigh and pour some wine into her favorite green glass and then go to put a Lean Cuisine in the microwave. Sadly, there aren't any left, but maybe she'll eat some actual food with calories instead, and that might give her the energy to sprint across the open fields yelling my name. Or else she'll just eat a salad and then wilt onto the couch, exhausted and weak, and fall asleep, the cats all piled up on her like she's their savior, which I guess she is, even if she's hardly ever home.

My stomach is grumbling, which means it must be pretty far past dinnertime now. I've lost track, I've lost time, I've lost everything that matters and I would kill for a stupid Lean Cuisine—that is, if I could use my arms. I can't kill anything while my arms are pinned to the walls of a well. Right now my own shoulder would probably taste good, even without bright orange, salty, sticky sauce on it.

The girls aren't coming back.

It's actually possible that I'll never be found. I'll be a mystery that you read about in the newspaper and sigh sadly to yourself while you chomp down a bowl of Cheerios, thinking about my young life, cut short so tragically. I hope they use my school picture from last year because it's my favorite. In it, my face is at an angle so you can't tell that my two front teeth overlap each other. And the way I'm kind of looking up a little bit, I look like maybe I'm shy, which I am, but I don't usually look the same way that I feel. I really love that picture because it looks like how I look in my head when I think about how I look, not like how I usually look in the mirror, which is freckled and pink-cheeked, like my skin is too many colors, like my face is louder than my soul.

I wonder what the headlines will say if they *do* find me, dead and gone, half-rotted with the goats. DEAD GIRL IN A WELL? GIRL IN WELL WITH DEAD GOATS? GIRL PERISHES IN WELL? THE GIRL FROM FAMILY OF LIARS DIES IN A WELL? GOATS, GIRL DEAD IN WELL. DAUGHTER

OF EMBEZZLER DEAD IN WELL. KARMA STRIKES BACK IN NOWHERESVILLE.

I wonder if Marianne Singleton will read about me to the whole class, who are now in sixth grade, just like me, but at my old school. I wonder if they will remember me. I wonder if anyone will cry. Maybe Tracy Kelliher will. She was my best friend right up until my dad was put away. Her dad is a policeman. Her dad took my dad to jail. I guess that's an important detail that I should have mentioned before. My bad.

The night before the arrest, Mr. Kelliher had been at a barbecue at our house. He'd eaten a steak (well done) and chewed with his mouth open. He'd made dumb jokes about baseball and farting. He'd dropped me and Tracy, one by one, off the diving board into the pool in our clothes while we screamed and laughed. Then he'd tried to do it to Robby, too, but Robby was almost as tall as him, and managed to push Mr. Kelliher in instead, raising his hands in a victory salute. But while his arms were still up, Dad pushed Robby in from behind.

Pretty soon everyone was fully dressed, in the pool, laughing like hyenas.

After Dad was arrested, Tracy Kelliher, my lifelong BFF, stopped talking to me at all, which was fine by me, because I didn't have anything left to say. Not to her. Not to anyone.

"HELP!" I shout because it's been a while since I shouted. "Oh help."

It's hopeless.

I am going to die.

"Goats," I say. "It's you and me."

They don't answer. Zombie goats are very unfriendly, as it turns out.

I'm about to close my eyes and breathe my last, when I hear voices.

Grown-up voices! Of people!

Oh, happy day! I'll be saved! Hurray! I'm so excited and so hungry and I have to pee so bad that I start crying and laughing and gulping and shouting, all at once, and the most terrible thing happens: a hot gush of liquid rushes down my leg, pooling in my remaining favorite shoe.

"Kammie!" shouts a voice that I don't know. "Kammie!"

I move my sodden foot from the rock that is holding me up and I slip down again, fast, but not as fast as a roller coaster, not as fast as going down the Matterhorn at Disneyland, which I went to during spring break with Tracy's family back when Mom and Dad could afford to buy me a plane ticket, back when Tracy wanted to invite me to Disneyland. Disneyland was so great. I wish I was there right now, cruising down the river on the jungle cruise, which might be the lamest ride, but it's 10,000 times better than being in a well with wet shorts and a soggy shoe and no skin left on my elbows.

"Helllloooooo!" shouts the voice from the top of the well.

"Hello," I say back, in a normal voice. I have dropped two or three more feet. Three feet is a lot when you are only four feet tall.

"I can't hear you!" he shouts.

"HELLO," I scream, snappily, like it's his fault that I'm trapped in a well that now stinks of my own pee. I'm dumb. I am the dumbest. I am captain Dumb on the S.S. *Dumb* and I've sunk into the Sea of Dumb, where I am dumbly drowning *in my own pee.* "I AM IN HERE!" I scream. "GET ME OUT! HELP ME!"

"WE ARE GOING TO SAVE YOU!" shouts the man. I can't tell who it is because it's so dark up there. I don't want to be in this well in the dark. Where is my mom anyway?

"WHERE IS MY MOM?" I yell. "I WANT MY MOM."

"I'M KANDICE'S DAD," he says and it takes me a minute to figure out that Kandice is Kandy. I've never met her dad. I knew he existed and he worked at the warehouse, I just never really bothered to complete the picture. I liked imagining her dadless and momless, raising herself, tough and not bothered by details like parents or homework.

Kandy's dad's head disappears and the pool of inky blue sky settles back into its job of filling up the space. It's my favorite shade of blue, that darkest blue of evening, right before the sky lets go of all color and sinks into holey blackness, the holes letting the stars shine through. This blue is the color of fireworks about to start.

Then Kandy's dad is back. "SOMEONE IS GOING TO CALL YOUR MOM! SHE'S COMING!" he says. "WE ARE GOING TO LOWER A ROPE!" He is talking very slowly, leaving big spaces between his words like I must need that pause so that I can figure out what each word is, one at a time, adding them all up at the end like a math problem to get to the sum.

"OK!" I yell. "OK! OK."

All this yelling is tiring me out so much that even though it seems like a pretty awkward time to take a nap, I close my eyes. The dark blue of the sky pulls a blanket over the silver of my bad dream and freckles me with stars. Something twinkles. "Oh, hello," I say, in my sleep. An animal jumps up and down in front of me, tugging my sleeve with its mouth. "Stop," I say. The goat eats my sleeve. His lips feel soft and strange against my cut-up arms.

And then, *bam*, the rope hits me squarely on the head.

"GRAB THE ROPE!" Kandy's dad shouts.

"I CAN'T," I shout back, my voice still thick from the dream, and from being clonked on the head. "MY ARMS ARE STUCK."

The rope stays where it is, resting on my head like an old man's hand. I preferred the coyote, but it helps that he wasn't real so didn't weigh anything. Also, he was better company.

"CAN YOU GRAB IT WITH YOUR MOUTH?" he says.

"WHAT?" I yell, even though I heard him. With my *mouth*? I saw that in the circus once, a girl swinging from a rope with her mouth. Though actually maybe that wasn't a rope, maybe it was her hair, and she wasn't holding on with her teeth, her hair was just really long and was attached to something at the other end. My hair would be useless for that now that it's not attached to my head, and it wouldn't be long enough anyway. Then I yell, "NO! I CAN'T."

"HANG ON, KIDDO!" he yells. There is a scuffling sound at the top of the well and the rope disappears.

"Bye rope," I whisper. *"Au revoir!"* I'm nervous to look up in case he drops it again and it lands in my eye, but I do anyway and I see Kandy peering back at me. She is so tiny and far away, like I'm seeing her with binoculars that I'm looking through backwards.

"HEYYYYYYYYYY!" she says. "UM, HI! HOW'S IT GOING?"

"WHAT?" I yell. "WHERE WERE YOU?"

"ARE YOU OK?" she shouts.

"NO," I shout back.

"OH," she says. "SORRY, IT'S JUST THAT I HAD TO HAVE DINNER. MACARONI. UGH."

"YOU HAD DINNER?" I yell. "YOU HAD MACARONI?"

"I HAD TO!" she says. "MY MOM SAID I HAD TO EAT! THEN I SAID, MOM, SERIOUSLY, KAMMIE FELL INTO A WELL! AND SHE KEPT LAUGHING, LIKE I WAS JOKING! AND I WAS

LIKE, I AM NOT JOKING! AND SHE WAS LIKE, EAT! ORPHANS ARE STARVING IN OTHER COUNTRIES! THERE ARE HUNGRY PEOPLE IN AMERICA, TOO, YOU KNOW! THE 99%! AND I WAS LIKE, MOM, WE ARE IN THE 99%. AND SHE GOT MAD SO I ATE AND THEN I HAD HOMEWORK! I HAD TO DO IT! THEN I WAS LIKE, YOU KNOW, FREAKED OUT THAT YOU WERE GOING TO DIE SO I STARTED TO CRY AND MOM SENT ME TO MY ROOM! AND THEN MANDY'S MOM CALLED MY MOM AND SAID THAT MANDY SAID THAT YOU WERE IN THE WELL AND THEN THEY CALLED SANDY'S MOM AND SHE ASKED SANDY AND SANDY WAS LIKE, YES, KAMMIE IS IN THE WELL! AND THEN THERE WAS ALL THIS RUNNING AROUND! AND SHOUTING! MOM WAS SO MAD BUT I TRIED TO TELL HER! SHE HADN'T HEARD OF YOU! SHE THOUGHT I MADE YOU UP! BUT IT ALL WORKED OUT BECAUSE NOW MY DAD AND ME ARE GOING TO RESCUE YOU!"

Her words tumble down onto me like pellets of hail, and dance in my hair like fleas having a circus on a dead goat. I try to sort them all out into sentences and then paragraphs so that I know what she means, what she's saying. My brain is humming more slowly than usual; it's like a lullaby with one note, slow and sad. It's hard to rev up when you're crushed under the weight of performing fleas in a cloud of noxious dead-goat fumes.

"I FEEL FUNNY," I shout and it's suddenly really true, like I feel like my head and body aren't quite attached properly and something is wrong, my batteries are winding down and my voice comes out squished and twisty as a soft ice cream. My skin has opened up where my freckles used to be and stars are shining out. They've probably been waiting in me all this time, and the dullness of them was just their shutters being closed. Now they are open, just like me. Kandy's face is gone from the dark blue hole and the stars float up and stick there, waving good-bye.

The smell is worse. The air is gone. I'm breathing something that isn't air. I can feel my lungs turning yellow and spongy, melting toffee-thick into some gaseous poison. I cough, but nothing happens, just a *whoof whoof* of air, leaving me. I'm dizzy. I'm so dizzy. She ate macaroni? My brain is macaroni, orange and overcooked, disintegrating on the plate of my skull. Macaroni is the food of despair and the color of wrinkled carrots and thin air.

"Star light, star bright, first star I see tonight, I wish I may, I wish I might, have the wish I wish tonight," I say or I think or both. I close my eyes and float my wish up there, blowing on it like a flea riding on a dandelion seed, wishing, of course, that I am not in a well.

"KAMMIE?" shouts a man's voice, which is coming from the floating head of Kandy's dad. "ARE YOU STILL OK?"

"I'm dreaming in a thickly dream," I try to yell, but it comes out quiet, like you'd expect when the air is curdled yogurt. Suddenly, the walls of the well are as cool as sheets that you slide your feet into after a hot day and find a patch that hasn't already been scorched by your sleeping heat.

The goats are rustling underneath me, so maybe after all, they aren't zombies. They would like to come out. Probably they dream of being Moroccan tree goats, climbing up to eat all those Argan seeds so they can poop them out again to make oil for shining hair. The Argan goats are the envy of the goat world. *"OU EST MOROCCO?"* I say to them, all slow motion, with the wrong syllables and things. They make goat sounds in return. They sound like tiny horses. I don't know what goats sound like. Do they whinny?

"Non, non," they say. *"Ou est la salle de bain?"*

"OK," I tell them. "Fine. Be that way." I think they are mad that I brought up Morocco, the land of tree goat dreams. I think they are making fun of me for peeing in my shoe. "There is no bathroom here, *mes amis*," I add, for good measure.

I want to tell Kandy's dad's floating face in the distance about the animals down here who all speak gently in French, but it feels like it doesn't matter now. I'm sleepy and I'm being rescued, so maybe it would be OK if I just closed my eyes again and so I do, I close them, and the dream folds over me like layers of paper being creased perfectly by a teacher's hands, and pretty soon it's going to be a peace dove and I'm going to fly away on it to our sister city in Japan. I wish I didn't feel so funny, but it's just part of the dream, after all, and I really miss my dad, that's not even a lie, raisin-souled liar that he is.

7

DREAMS

I wake up, stiff and sore and still in the well. It's
been five minutes or five hours or five years. Maybe
I am fifteen now. Is it over?

"Dad?" I say.

And then from down deep below me, I hear my
dad's voice saying, "Sugar Peanut Pie, you're going
to have to wake up." Which is when I realize that
Dad has tunneled out of jail using salsa to melt
the metal bars and a spoon for digging, and he's
going to crawl up and save me. We saw that on

Mythbusters once, Dad and me, lying on the couch in the living room, me upside down, and him the right way up. Him saying, "If I'm ever in the slammer, I'll know what to do!" And me saying, "Salsa gives me a rash." And him laughing. And me laughing because neither of us ever imagined he'd be in prison, except he must have, because how could he not? He knew what he was doing.

"Au secours, Papa!" I whisper. "Help me!" and my whisper gets bigger as it falls down the well, until it is as big as a paper airplane, swooping into Dad's eye.

"Ouch!" he says. "Careful, sport."

A dog barks. It's nice that Dad has a dog, who is Lassie. *"Le woof,"* says the dog and I smile beatifically, which is a way of smiling that is very holy and nearly biblical and then, once again, something hard and heavy lands on my head. I have to swim through water and thick fog to get to the top of my own head, much like in the book *James and the Giant Peach* where they eat their way to the surface of the peach, only to find they are on the ocean. I eat my way to the surface of me. On my head, there is a tube that is blowing cold air.

"*Zut alors, Papa!*" I say. "Lassie, *quelle heure est-il?*"

"*Le woof*," says the dog sadly.

Dad says, "Do you hear music? I love this song."

"But you have terrible taste," I say. "What song is this?"

"It's that kid," he says. "Rory Darren? The one with the bad hair."

"He doesn't sing, mostly he just meows," I say. "And it's *Devon*." My dad laughs because I'm the funniest and my head is blocking the TV and no one can see whether the thing about the salsa is a myth or if it's really going to work next time one of us needs to bust our way to freedom.

I look up at the hole at the entrance to my freedom, which is bruised with night now, black and final, an abyss or a black hole or both. There are two new faces up there, both wearing large red hats. Santa! No, wait, they are cartoon firemen, which must mean it is Saturday morning and I am on the

rec room floor with Robby, arguing over which cartoon to watch, but where are my Froot Loops?

"THIS IS UNACCEPTABLE!" I shout, which
isn't what comes out of my mouth, but never mind.
Glarg, glarg. Words mean more than you want them
to most of the time, or less, but never the right
amount.

"KAMMIE," shouts a man in a red hat with a
light on it, which is the light at the end of the tunnel, which means he is probably God or maybe a
coal miner. If so, he took a wrong turn. This is a
warehouse town! No one mines anymore. Or if they
do, they don't do it here. They must. Somewhere,
someone is a miner, down there in the tunnels in
the dark. Poor man.

"KAMMIE," says the man again. I bet he wishes
he'd taken a job at the warehouse instead, even
though those jobs are terrible and Mom's feet are
lumpy with raw blisters from all the walking and
running she does all day long to meet the one-day
delivery promises made by the company. "KAMMIE,
YOU HAVE TO TRY TO ANSWER."

My name, Kammie, is very strange. Listen to the two syllables: *Kam. Me.*

"AMEN!" I mumble-shout because that sounds like the password into Heaven. How do dying people remember what to say? I hope Dad can come, too, and his little French lass, Doggie, and even the goat zombies, who are now like brothers to me, I call them Robby Robby and Le Robby-Robby.

"ROBBY!" I say, which is also not really a winner, being *Rob* and *Bee*. *I went on a robbing bee, and I took all the money.* You have to sing it with money having three syllables instead of two. Like mu-uh-nee. Try it.

"KAMMIE," the man shouts again. "THIS IS SERIOUS. WE THINK YOU MIGHT BE RUNNING OUT OF OXYGEN DOWN THERE AND THE TUBE ON YOUR HEAD HAS OXYGEN. YOU NEED TO GET IT INTO YOUR MOUTH AND THEN TRY TO BREATHE ONLY THROUGH YOUR MOUTH. DO YOU UNDERSTAND? IT'S LIKE DRINKING FROM A STRAW."

I hear, "Oxygen oxygen oxygen." Everyone

wants me to put things in my mouth. Haven't they heard of hygiene? Hygiene and oxygen are both words that are made of silk yarn. My brain tries to weave that into a scarf. It doesn't work. Why? It's a straw! This hatted man-angel, unemployed coal miner must think I'm very dumb, but he doesn't know I have the brain power of all of us in the well. I am pulling more and more power in through my one bare foot, which is sadly now being nibbled by a crab who would prefer peaches. We can't all be a peach. My name is Kammie. Kammie is peachy keen. I like saying peachy keen. I think I used to say it all the time. Tracy would say, "Do you like my new haircut?" And I'd say, "It's so peachy keen." This book is peachy keen. This show is peachy keen. How was school? Peachy keen. It's an old fashioned thing to say. Grandma loved saying peachy keen. Her cookies were peachy keen. I need Grandma's Peachy Keen Cookie Recipe! How else will I bring Grandma back?

I am bringing *peachy keen* back, lovingly wrapping the words up and dropping them carefully into modern times like the past itself is lobbing gifts into the future, through me.

The man keeps saying, "KAMMIE! YOU HAVE TO PUT IT IN YOUR MOUTH. YOU HAVE TO BREATHE IT IN."

The man is magic! He isn't a god or an angel! He's a *magician*. Little white rabbits are pouring out of his hat and landing on my head with the fleas and the silver coyote. This could be an emergency, but the man is right that I am so thirsty. My mouth is sand and dirt, like the rest of this state. I sip from the straw, but there isn't anything in the straw! It's a joke. A terrible joke.

I try to breathe through the straw because the man is getting upset. His frustration is alive, a tiny fish, flicking its fins at me. It feels pleasantly weird to drink from it! Try it if you can. I'm drinking silver air. I thought I didn't like silver, but maybe I do because it tastes cold and smooth, like something blended with ice and mixed with clouds. Bronze air would taste like gravy. I hang for a while, dangling, the crab still clinging to my foot, drink-breathing all that metallic wonder and after a few minutes I start to remember that I am stuck in a well. Worse, my dad is gone. He was here! Except he wasn't here. My dad is in jail, miles away, saving up his salsa. Are they allowed to watch *Mythbusters* in prison?

The man in the hat is a fireman.

"KEEP BREATHING," he calls. "YOU'LL FEEL BETTER IN A FEW MINUTES."

He's right, I do feel better. I also feel worse. I can feel the cuts on my arms and legs, the plink-plonk of bleeding coming from somewhere on my shin. It feels burned and black, like charred toast. The blood is the jam. I'm hungry. I'm thirsty. I'm freezing. My goosebumps have goosebumps, like those drawings of stairs that just go up and up and up forever, they're like that, goosebumps with no end. I'm vibrating with cold. Record players work because the needle reads the vibration of the grooves on the vinyl disc. That's a cool fact, told to me by Record Store Dave. The needle is made from a real diamond crystal.

"Are you cold?" I want to ask the goats, but

I can't. My voice is gone in a grain of sand that's fallen out of my mouth and landed on a beach.

Up above me, I can hear lots of voices now, more and more, like there is a parade or a party.

"KAMMIE," someone shouts.

It's Robby, so I let the straw fall out of my mouth and scream, "DON'T YOU DARE SPIT!" Nothing comes out. Oh well. What I meant was, "Robby! Help me!"

Robby and I used to be really good friends. When we were little, we used to do everything together. We made up games. We pretended to be everyone and everything that wasn't us and sometimes climbed trees. We built a tree house in our old backyard out of scrap lumber that the guy at Home Depot gave to us. The tree house was crooked. If you sat on one side, you practically tipped right out of the tree. The danger is what made it fun, we agreed. Mom and Dad did not agree and forbade us from going into it. Dad was going to "tear it out of there before someone gets killed." Well, he didn't do it. He often forgot to bother with following up. Robby and I used it all the time anyway. From up there, we could see into everyone else's backyards. We could see Tommy Hennessy picking his nose and eating it. We could see April and Tawny Smythe pretending to be runway models wearing bedsheets and wigs from their mom's hair place. We could see all the people who we were glad not to be. Back then, it was good to be Robby and me, me and Robby, in our safely dangerous house in the tree.

Then Robby turned 14 and got annoyed with everyone and everything. "Stop being annoyed," I'd say, and he'd say, "I'm not annoyed, I'm really mad. I'm mad at you." He knew I hated it when anyone was mad at me, but it didn't matter because he was 14 and straight-up always mad. Not just at me, but at everyone and everything. Sometimes he was so mad, his face erupted with white pustules of bad moods, waiting to be burst, leaving gross marks on the mirror. When those zits are all gone, I figure he'll be Robby again. The nice one, not the luck hog. Not the great debater. Not the door-slamming, Kammie-hating, Dad-defender who he is now. He defends Dad all the time. He says, "Dad is a good person who made a mistake, Kammie." He says, "It's sort of your fault. You kept asking him for more stuff."

"KAMMIE," he yells right now at this exact minute, to me in the well. "GET OUT OF THE WELL. GET OUT OR I'M GOING TO BE MAD AT YOU."

"Ha ha," I say, which comes out like this, "Haaaaa."

"MADE YOU LAUGH," he booms. *Boom, boom, boom.*

"It's Dad's fault." I feel like somehow Robby can hear me, even though I didn't really say that.

"He didn't mean to," Robby says, as if he is speaking inside my head. "He only wanted the best for you. You kept asking for more stuff! All those American Girl dolls!"

"I don't even like them!" I try to say, but my voice is being absorbed by my coyote friend. "I just liked the catalogue. Stop saying this stuff to me. It isn't my fault." I start to cry.

"KAMMIE," he bellows. "I WON'T BE MAD IF YOU GET OUT OF THE WELL."

"I can't," I say or don't say. "That's not fair. I'm frogging in the well's throat." This makes perfect sense to me, but he can't hear it. I don't have a microphone. So *boom, boom, boom* to you, too.

Then he spits. I hear it. I think I hear it. Maybe he doesn't. I think he does. My hair is already so full of fleas and spiders and Mandy/Kandy/Sandy's gum. I've forgotten whose gum it is. It doesn't matter. All three of them are the same jaw, chewing.

"YOU SPAT IN MY HAIR!" I try to yell, but still nothing. Maybe something. Air. Silver air. Leaking up the mine shaft into his eyes. *Boom*. Take that. His eyes, frozen by my airy words, land on my head like Ping-Pong balls and then bounce back up again to his face. My poor head. My poor hair. Poor me, all over.

"SHE SEEMS OK TO ME," he yells. "AT LEAST SHE'S FINALLY SHUT UP FOR TWO MINUTES IN A ROW." He makes a raspberry sound and shout-whispers into the microphone, "WE HAD CHICKEN FOR DINNER AND I GOT THE WISHBONE, DUMBO. IT WAS REAL CHICKEN. LIKE, A ROTISSERIE ONE."

And so I'm like, "THAT'S JUST LOVELY, JERK-FACE." Still nothing. (Or maybe a whisper, a bone that's stuck in my throat, a rasping gate. Dying is such a quiet thing. I'd have thought it would be noisier.)

Then he's gone and Mom is up there. "Kammie?" she says, like we're talking on the phone. "Hello?" Mom doesn't like talking into things. Once Dad used his iPhone to record us on Christmas morning opening our presents. She nearly went nuts. She kept starting to say things and freezing up and panicking because it was being filmed.

"Oh, this is so lovely! It's just so . . . oh, I forgot that thing was on. Is it on?" The video is full of Dad pointing the phone at her and asking, "What present did you just open? Who was it from?" And her ducking her head with her wet-wool whispers,

"I can't! I can't!" Then you see me grinning and hear me squealing about my new skates, and you hear Robby going, "Cooooool" when he opens his electric guitar.

That was a good year. It was the last good year. It snowed all day and all night, and we spent the whole week between Christmas and New Year's sledding down the back lawn and skating on the few inches of ice in the bottom of the pool that Dad called a homemade rink. "Think of all that money we could save if you just skated here instead of at the rink, kiddo," he said to me. "Think of it!" I'm thinking of it now. I wonder how much he stole to pay Coach Martine to teach me how to do a camel spin, which I hated doing. The spins made me dizzy. I didn't ever want to tell anyone that though. It sounded ungrateful. Skating lessons were expensive. "Future Olympian," Dad called me, on those early mornings when we drove to my extra lessons, my breath steaming up the window enough that I could make smileys with my finger on the glass.

"Mommy," I say, like someone asleep, murmuring out of a dream. I don't call her Mommy. Not ever. Well, maybe when I'm sick. "Mom."

She raises her voice just a bit. "TALK TO ME, HONEY!" she says. "ARE YOU OK?"

"OF COURSE NOT!" is what I want to say, full blast, blowing her out of the opening and up into the night sky. "NO!" I say, but what comes out of my mouth is more like the sound of something quiet, trying to hide in a shadow under a door. A mouse. The word *mouse* comes from a word in another language, I forget which one, that means "thief." Mice are thieves. My dad is a mouse. I fish around with my mouth for the straw again and concentrate on drinking air. It blows wind into my mouth, which is a desert, which creates a sandstorm, which makes me wheeze.

Mom's so far away, staring down at me, like she can't believe what she's doing, lying on her belly in a field, staring down a hole at her second-born child, deciding whether to be mad or sad. She's so tiny up there, I don't even know if I can see her or if I can just imagine her there.

"HOW MANY TIMES . . ." she starts, then she stops. She's shouting into the microphone! Isn't she afraid of it? My mom is afraid. So you are not my mommy. The person who is not my mommy is crying rain. I know she is because it's raining on my head. It can't be. I'm out in space and tears dissolve in space or they float the wrong way. They go up. My tears are splashing Mom's face. I look past her face and into the night, searching for stars, only they are gone. "I LOVE YOU, OK, BYE," she says finally, and then she's gone to stir some more hopes, and there is a man who I don't know and he's saying, "We're dropping a hose, this one has water, you need to drink water." I nod and smile, yes, thank you! Water! This idea is terrific! I am so thirsty!

The hose bounces down and dribbles water on me. My eyes start to leak, tears all blurred with the rain because my body doesn't know that I don't have any water in me to spare. I grapple around with my mouth for the end of the hose. I'm getting shockingly good at that. *Throw the rope now*, I want to say. *I'll catch it in my mouth.* I drink and drink and drink, like I'm filling myself back up, but then I stop because what if I overinflate? Then they won't be able to pull me out if they try. I'll be too big.

The water tastes like when you are outside playing, too lazy to go inside, and you gulp water from the hose. It tastes like rubber and metal and dirt and something like swimming pool chemicals, and it tickles the back of your throat in a way that makes you not quite feel sick. I wish I was drinking from the hose with Tracy Kelliher and getting water all over our clothes and then laying out towels on the lawn to lie on so we get hot in the sun before plunging back into the ice-cold pool. Sometimes our moms would sit out there too, on lawn chairs, slathered all over with SPF 1000 suntan lotion so they didn't get skin cancer and die. That was back when avoiding cancer seemed smarter than smoking, for Mom. Summer smells like SPF and pool chlorine and lawn chairs and pages of magazines stuck together with damp hands. But it *tastes* like water from this plastic hose. I start to cry again. It's so dark. I'm so dark. My stars have clouded over. I'm my own raincloud.

They are up top, being busy. *They* are going to do something. *They* are going to save me. I don't know if I want that. Grandma was going to do it. I hope she comes soon. Maybe I could go to her instead. Heaven sounds like a warm place with counters low enough that I can stir the batter. With a fancy mixer, of course. Mixing is hard on the arms and I don't seem to have any. Grandma and I will make cookies. Chewy and chocolate-y. Yes, please. Peachy keen. The edges kind of crunchy and hardened from the oven and the middle bits still gooey and hot.

I go back to the air and breathe deep. I pretend that I'm snorkeling. Look at that piece of coral! Look at that turtle! I have never been snorkeling, not even once, but Tracy Kelliher went to Hawaii at Christmas last year and didn't invite me. She fed bright yellow fish frozen peas and they nibbled at her fingers. When she told me that, I started screaming. Still, Hawaii sounded fun with all the hula dancing and a big pig roast where people played the ukulele and juggled with fire, turtles snapping at your ankles.

"KAMMIE?" the voices above me boom. They are God. God is booming at me. I croak out a sound that sounds like "Frrrg" and the voices say, "ARE YOU THERE? STAY WITH US. WE ARE GOING TO START DIGGING, OK?"

"OK?" What do I know about whether digging is a good idea or not? Doesn't God have a good handle on their own good ideas? Or bad? I want to go home. I want to get into my bed. I want Robby to fart in his bed and then fan it at me so that I can squeal and throw something at him and he can throw something back and Mom can come and stand in the doorway, leaning sideways, her eyes not quite focused because she's so tired and we should just let her sleep, but for some reason we can't. And she'll say, "Stop that. You guys. Come on."

It doesn't sound that great, but trust me, when compared to being stuck in a well, it's paradise.

The water keeps pouring out of the hose and down my back. I'm so cold. I feel like even if I could move, I couldn't. I wish, I wish, I wish I was warm.

When Dad used to work, he worked at a place called Dreams Come True. It was where sick kids submitted their wishes and then people donated money, and the money bought their wishes for them. It worked best when the kid wished for Disneyland, which pretty much every kid did. The thing with all the kids is that they had cancer and they weren't going to live. I guess some of them did, but not all of them. If they lived, it was a miracle and they got to be in the ads for Dreams Come True talking about how they were sick and got a wish and then they got better. It sort of implied that the wish made them live, which made me feel weird, because it was a lie. What made them better was medicine and good luck and maybe a miracle. Not a ride on Big Thunder Mountain. They got better because they were lucky.

I didn't like to be around those kids too much because I felt bad for being so alive, for feeling good, for not looking like I was going to just keel over and flat-out die right then and there in the front office of the foundation. And my Dad was taking money from those kids! He was doing that! At least, that's how people saw it, the ones who saw the story on the news, everyone who read one of the kajillion articles on the Internet, anyone who loves to get morally outraged about someone else's terrible mistake. In other words, everyone.

One day after that first front-page article was printed, Mom and I were at the Shop Rite buying eggs and butter and milk and a new box of laundry soap, and an old lady came up to Mom and said, "You should be ashamed of yourself." She said it so casually it was like she was saying, "That brand of butter is better than this one." Like she wasn't going to cripple us with her words—or kill us, really. My mom already mostly dead from the heartbreak of it all. Like this lady wasn't going to be the last straw.

Mom held the laundry soap in her arms like she was cradling a baby and then the lady really lit into her. She grabbed Mom's arm and the laundry soap-baby fell screaming to the floor and the box split open, so all this white soap powder was everywhere, smelling so strong that my eyes stung, or maybe I was crying. "My granddaughter died!" she yelled. "She died! She had the cancer in her blood and she died! And before she died, she made a wish, she wanted to go to Disneyland! But she didn't get to go! She didn't get to go because she died! Your husband took that money from my granddaughter. You are terrible." Her hand was so white against Mom's denim jacket and the veins in her hands looked like a map, where if you started tracing them, you could easily follow them all the way back to that lady's broken heart.

By then I was crying, because it's so sad when kids die of cancer, especially when they didn't get to go to Disneyland, after all. I went to Disneyland. Why did I get to go? Dad probably paid with the money this woman's grandkid could have used. The lady whirled around on me and she said, "Is this his kid? The child of that devil? She's evil, too, I'm betting. She's evil because she has his rotten, no-good blood flowing through her veins. It should be kids like her that get cancer, that die. You should die!" she yelled. She yelled it so close to me that I could see the bumps on her tongue, the way her too-orange make-up had fallen into the creases on her face.

"I'm sorry," I whispered, and Mom pulled me into her body, clutching me against her belly.

"That is a terrible thing to say to this child, this innocent child. This child didn't do anything! I'm sorry about your granddaughter but you can't say those things!" she shouted back at that woman, stomping her feet a bit so the soap rose up in clouds.

The woman blinked, like she'd just woken up from being asleep. She didn't say anything, just let out a slow hiss like a balloon breathing out all the exhalations it was holding in. She hated me. I know that. I know she was looking at me and seeing her poor dead granddaughter, and all over again, I hated my dad so much, more than anything, more than anyone. I was passing on the hate, like pass the parcel. The music is playing. Open the present! Here is some hate.

My mom's body was shaking behind me, an earthquake I couldn't pull away from. We went home without the groceries. Mom drove slowly, clutching the steering wheel so hard her fingers were white as the bones that were in them, right there under her skin.

"We'll pay it back," she murmured, her teeth clenched so hard I could hardly understand her. "I'll pay it back."

But I know she can't. She can't ever. It was so much money. She'll never be able to make it right.

And neither will I.

Not ever.

Not even if I get cancer and all my hair falls out and I die.

Not even if I die right here in this well, the sandpapery walls of it scratching at my skin like they are coming to life and rubbing the layers right off my shivering body. I am suddenly remembering to be scared. And I am scared. I am so scared.

"Mom?" I say, but she can't hear me. "I don't want to die."

But boy, if I do die, that old lady will be happy, I think. That old lady will be able to sleep at night, knowing that balance has been restored. But I guess it still wouldn't be fair, because I *did* get to go to Disneyland. I did get to live that dream.

8

NORTh DaKota

Mandy is at the top of the well, talking into the microphone. I'm allowed to call her Mandy now, I guess. But I don't want to call her Mandy. I don't want to call her anything. I want to hang up the phone, but it isn't a phone. I can't hang up.

I stare at the well wall in front of me, which is like looking into a shadow to try and find a light. There's nothing there. Well, there's something there. Grains of dirt, squashed together to make clay bricks. I picture them each individually, floating apart and setting me free. There are probably people who could do that with their brains, like ESP, but different. Those people are probably monks. Monks probably very rarely fall down wells in Texas.

I close my eyes. Mandy keeps talking. "So, like, in the club, we have rules? And you have to know what they are? So while you are down there, you can memorize them? I'll tell you that the first rule is that you aren't allowed to tell anyone that this is a club and that this was, um, part of anything." She's sort of whispering, sort of shouting. I hope there are crowds of firemen up there, eavesdropping. I hope Robby hears her and punches her in the nose. I hope my mom hears her.

"Um, the second rule is that you have to wear only Smash Hit perfume, OK? You have to also do your hair in a certain different braid every day, like Monday is fishtail and Tuesday is French ... Oh, um, forget it. Your hair is too short. You'll have to, basically, grow out your hair." Her voice is sing-songy and strange. Is she talking about braids?

My head is shivering. My head is a baby bird

without any feathers, all pink and vulnerable to eagle attacks. What if an eagle swoops into the well and begins pecking at my head? I don't like birds much more than fish, if I'm being honest.

". . . Um, and then we can dip the ends of our braids in Kool-Aid powder to make colors, but we only do that on Fridays because it's fun day on Friday."

Between Mandy's sentences, I can hear the *chukka chukka chukka* sound of shovels hitting the dirt and then a bigger sound, like an engine roaring, the ground caving in under its weight. Something is caving in. I am caving in. Mandy's voice is caving in. There's another voice. It's Mandy. No, it's Robby. It's Robby. Robby is saying, "Shut up, Mandy." Robby is saying, "Hey, Kammie? Mandy is a freak. You shouldn't be friends with her. OK, I'm going to tell you a joke now. This is the joke. Knock knock." He pauses. The pause stretches over me like a bubble gum bubble. It's all around me. Then it caves in, just like everything is caving in right now. The cave! The cave!

I was in a cave once. I forget where we were. Camping, I think, in Upstate New York. Dad used to like to just drive and drive and we'd be looking down, watching movies on the iPad or playing our DS3s and then before we knew it, we'd left New Jersey somewhere behind us in a cloud of Costcos and Bed Bath and Beyonds, and we were somewhere with forests or fields or beaches or lakes, and it felt like we'd driven right off the planet and landed somewhere better. This time I'm thinking of, it was crazy hot and the cave was dark and cool. Robby and I were hiding. We could hear Mom and Dad calling us and then we heard Mom swear and Dad laughing and them deciding we were either dead or joking, and Dad saying, "Well, if they're dead, I call the top bunk!"

We used to share a bed on trips back then, before Robby started bringing a tent and putting it beside the truck so he didn't have to get anywhere near me. He said I farted in my sleep, which wasn't even true. He said I drooled. He said he wouldn't be surprised if I peed. He said I was gross.

Mom said, "Don't worry, sweetie, he's a teenager."

And I said, "I'm never going to be a teenager, then, because teenagers are lying liars who lie." That was before I knew that everyone lied, everyone over the age of 11, anyway. And even then, I'm not so sure. Mandy, Kandy, and Sandy aren't exactly paragons of the truth. They aren't grapes. They are raisins.

"Kammie," Robby yells. "You have to say, 'Who's there?' or else this joke doesn't ever end."

"Who's there," I say, but my voice is flat coins that clink to the bottom of the well. "I wish I was free," I say, but it's just more coins, falling on the goats and all around.

The cave we found on that trip was cold and the walls sweated this cool water that was really salty if you tasted it, which I did, not because I'm gross but because Robby dared me. The top of the cave was so high that it looked like the black night sky, even though it was day. It wasn't until after that I found out that it was black because of the bats. The ground was thick with gunk. I should have guessed what that was, but I didn't. Instead, Robby and I just pressed our backs against that wet cave wall and crouched behind a stalactite or a stalagmite, I forget which, and giggled. Then I accidentally stepped on his foot, so he pushed me and I landed head first on the stalactite/stalagmite and he had to run and get Mom and Dad. Right up until this exact second, I thought that those ten minutes I was alone in that cave were the most terrifying ten minutes of my life.

Wrong.

"INTERRUPTING CHICKEN," yells Robbie now, scaring me. "That only works if you had said 'Who's there,'" he says. "You wrecked the joke."

I had to get three stitches in my forehead from the stalagmite/stalactite wound. I wonder if they'll be able to sew me up again after this. I wonder if I'll look like a rag doll. I wonder if all my blood has leaked out.

I slip again. See? I'm shrinking.

"I'm shrinking," I say to Robby, but Mandy is talking again.

"Your brother is a pig," she says.

"Robby?" I say.

"He's the worst. Anyway, in the summer," she hits that word hard, like it matters, "we're going to use lemons to dye our hair blonde, all of us. I guess you could do that, too, even though your hair is so short."

No, I want to say, but don't. *No, I'm not your friend. No, I won't be blonde. No, in the summer, I won't know you anymore because I'll be gone.*

Where am I going?

Where do dead people go?

Am I dying?

I've forgotten. I'm feeling funny again, confused. There is more grinding and the earth is giving way.

I wish there was music. Someone needs to pipe in music. If I could have music, I think I would pick Simon and Garfunkel. Record Shop Dave played me their music last Tuesday when I stopped by on the way home from school. It was really good music. Their voices were like metal, twisting together and rising up, washing all over me and cooling off my

hottest heart. I felt like I never wanted to stop listening to those songs. Dave gave me the album and
I took it home because I was too embarrassed to
tell him that I didn't have anything I could play it
on. I'm saving up for a record player. Dave has one
for sale in his store that I love—it is red and shiny
and has a handle. From the outside, it looks like a
perfect, square suitcase. But on the inside, there's
that needle with the diamond nestled inside, waiting to sing.

In the meantime, I stuck the record under my
mattress, and sometimes I dream the songs. Maybe
Robby will find it. I guess it will probably be cracked,
two black pieces of plastic that can't be glued back
together again to make the sound of the song that
could have saved me. I hope he puts it under his
mattress. I hope he dreams my old music dream because then he won't think I'm gross anymore and
he'll like me again like he used to. And maybe when
he's dead, too, he'll find me in Heaven or wherever
and it will be like it was before, when there was
nothing better in the world than jumping off an old

wharf into a cold lake on a hot summer day with his kid sister, who he didn't hate yet.

"And every Tuesday, you have to bring the snack, like maybe something nonfat or diet because we don't want to get fat," Mandy says.

I hate Mandy. The hate is in a parcel that I'm passing, but when I feel my hands, there is nothing in them, so I must have dropped it. Maybe Dad caught it. Maybe he hates Mandy, too. Was it Mandy or Kandy or Sandy who thought falling down a well was a good idea? Let's just gather round and hate them all and their nonfat snacks. I don't have any money. Mom doesn't have any money. I don't want to go to Mandy/Kandy/Sandy meetings! What might they do to me next? They will feed me to the fishes. Will there be a record player that I can use in Heaven? I hope it is red.

The walls below me are sweating with my blood. It's creepy. I want to go home. The bats are starting to stir.

The machine opens its mouth and takes a huge bite of the ground somewhere above me or beside me, I can't tell which. It chews and chews. Mandy is wearing a hard hat. "I have to go," she says. "They say it's, like, not safe. Bye for now!" She talks like she is hanging up the phone.

"Good-bye," I say, and my invisible voice is a ghost of smoke. Smoke is fire that has died. It makes sense. Think about it.

Mandy, Kandy, and Sandy are going to want to be my best friends after this because I will be famous. But I will say, "No" if I get to live and make the choice. If I don't live, they will answer questions on the TV news. They'll lie and say they loved me, even as they shrink into raisins.

If I die, they'll put teddy bears at the top of the well. They'll sprinkle flower petals down on me and the goats like rain, and the fleas will catch them and eat them, and the coyote will say, wisely, "These girls were never your friends!" And I will nod, sagely, in my white ghostly dress and say, "Yes, yes, yes, but now I can haunt them." I will haunt them with bad hair. I will stick things in their perfect braids while they sleep, like chewed gum and the poop of a goat.

If I get to be alive, I am going to be best friends with the girls with the glasses and bad hair and weird clothes and the limps. I am going to find the kids who are like me, skating champions who happen to love the sounds of silence and music playing loud in a car roaring down a highway toward a place where it snows, a place that is real, not a dusty, dry dream.

I wish I wasn't so sleepy. Once before, I was this sleepy. I can tell the story now because I have time and because no one is listening. It happened in September. September, last year. What happened was this. I'll summarize the whole thing in case you weren't paying attention to details before. Mostly, people don't pay attention to details until after something happens, then they look back in their memories for details, but memories are often pretty faulty, so if you're making up my story, you're going to get it wrong. Here it is again, in bullet points. (I don't know what bullet points are, but dad used to say it a lot: "Bullet points: chores are beds, baths, boogers." That meant, make your bed, clean the bathroom, and never leave the house without checking your nose for boogers.)

Bullet points of my life: My dad went to jail for robbing sick kids of their chance to have breakfast with Mickey Mouse, and my mom got two jobs in Texas, and my brother stopped talking to me, and our dog, Hayfield, got run over by the number 12 bus right in front of the house, and my former best friend, Tracy Kelliher, said loudly to Sarah Moore that that was karma. That's the end of the bullet points.

Here are the details: After that happened, the thing with Hayfield and Tracy and what she said, I started peeing in my bed every night. I don't know why I did that. I'd go to bed thirsty and wake up in a puddle of pee. I had to wear a diaper. "Diaper baby," Robby would hiss at me, over our micro-waved dinners. "Princess Baby Diaper of Diaper City, Diaper State, Diaperland." The house ran out of air and nice smells. We were turning moldy, like a loaf of bread left somewhere wet.

I didn't want to be me anymore. It seemed like it would be better to just not *be* at all. I wanted to die. That's what I'm saying.

So I did this thing. I'm embarrassed now. Even thinking about it makes me feel funny and light, like that time I plugged in the Christmas tree lights and didn't notice that the dog had chewed the cover off the wire and I got a shock that glued me in place, filling me with a trembling light, like my heart was feathers.

This is the thing that I did: I waited till everyone was out of the house. Mom was picking up Robby, who had been caught shoplifting at the Shop Rite. I wanted to know what he stole but I also wanted to be dead more than I cared if it was a Coke or a Pepsi. Lately he'd started saying he liked Pepsi better. We'd always been a Coke family. Maybe he took one of each. Maybe he couldn't decide and took a Dr. Pepper instead. I cared, but I also didn't. Not enough.

Anyway, I didn't want to live in a world that would run over Hayfield. I didn't want to have chafing on the top of the insides of my legs because I was always peeing in my bed. I wanted a mom. And a dad. My mom and *my* dad, the way they were before everything happened and their souls raisined and they went bad. The bad guys were my parents. You have to understand.

I called a number. I used the phone in Mom and Dad's room. It was a really super old phone that Mom had had in her house when she was a kid. She used to be a very sentimental person. Our house was a museum of her life. Dad happened to live there, too, but everything that mattered was Mom's. Like that phone. And my water bed. The phone plugged into the wall and the receiver was separate from the phone and really heavy. It made it feel real and solid, what I was doing. I pressed the numbers one at a time and it made a very satisfying *BEEP-BEEP* sound each time. The number I called was a help line, said the ad on the wall at school. You could call it and ask for help. I wanted someone to help me un-be. I wanted someone to get that. No one I knew would get it. I mean, they wanted me to un-be, too, but probably not in an easy, painless way. Definitely not in an easy, painless way. They wanted me to get cancer, specifically. And then radiation and chemo, and then a bald head. Well, if they could see me now, I guess they'd be happy.

Anyway, I dialed the number and then I hung up. I needed to pee first. So I went into Mom's bathroom to pee. The mirror in there was all covered with toothpaste spit. I couldn't imagine her brushing so energetically that she sprayed the mirror. It was like her limbs barely worked since Dad was taken away. That spray made me hesitate for a whole minute, thinking about Mom and how she was being pretty brave, considering, and pretending to be cheerful when she obviously wasn't, and brushing her teeth so hard it sprayed. But then I realized it was probably old. Maybe even from Dad. He was always brushing his teeth like it was his full-time job. He looked like a rabid dog. It was truly disgusting, all that gobby toothpaste foam that he made. Thinking about it now makes me want to be sick. Back then, I almost barfed, too. Thinking about Dad had that effect on me.

I opened the door of the medicine cabinet, and inside there were about ten bottles of pills. They were all different sizes and all in different amber bottles with cotton balls stuffed in the top. I took out all the cotton balls and sniffed them. I like the way cotton balls smell, OK? Also the way they feel against your skin, like rabbits and something gentle. On the side of the sink was a mug with a happy face on it that said NORTH DAKOTA. I put some water in the mug and drank it and wondered if any of those pills would make me un-be. We didn't bring the mug when we moved. Maybe we should have moved to North Dakota instead. Mom went to North Dakota on a school exchange when she was fifteen. That's what the mug was from. She said it was nice. I said, "Was it happy?" And she said, "There were a lot of trees." Like she didn't understand the question. "But were you happy there?" I asked. "Sure," she said. "I've always been happy." Well, that was before the thing with Dad. Mom didn't make the mug, it came from there, so maybe North Dakota is famous for happiness. I wish we'd picked there. Well, anyway, the mug got left behind. Just like the happiness.

I took the mug of water back to the bedroom. The water tasted funny, like soap, but that was OK. It reminded me of when I was little and Dad would get me a glass of water in the middle of the night, and he always got it from the bathroom and it always tasted just like this. I guess when people wash their hands, soap must get on the underside of the tap and flavor the water somehow. I sipped and dialed again. The hard *beep-beep-beep* of the numbers was the right thing to do. I knew it.

Finally, a man came on the phone. It sounded like my dad. So I was like, "Dad?" And he said, "My name is Des, how can I help you? What's your name?" And I said, "I'm not comfortable calling you that, can I call you Mr. Des?" And he said, "Yes, OK. No problem." So then I asked him if any of the pills in the medicine cabinet in Mom's bathroom could make me un-be. And he said, "What is un-be, darling?" And I got frosty with him because "darling" was too familiar and I said, "It's none of your business, really, Mr. Des, but seeing as you asked, I'm wondering if there is some sort of a pill for doing suicide." And I heard him pull in his breath, fast and sharp, like a bus slamming on its brakes right before the *bang* that says it has hit your dog. Then I hung up.

I wound the weird, long, curly cord from the phone around my fingers a few times, so my fingers were gone. I wanted to wrap it around my whole body but it wasn't long enough, just long enough for the fingers. Then I drank the water for a little while and watched the sunlight filter through the window. It lit up all this dust in the air. If you looked close, the dust looked like very tiny hairs. The bus went by outside. The Number 7. *I could go out there*, I thought. *I could just cross the road, like Hayfield was doing. Then I'd un-be.* I thought that and then I got sleepy. I got sleepy and I dreamed that I walked out onto the front lawn and the bus stopped and I got on and it drove away. In the dream, I was holding the happy mug. It was a good dream. I seriously thought I had solved some kind of very important problem.

Of course! I could always get on the bus!

I woke up when the door to Mom and Dad's bedroom slammed open. It was the police. Well, it was Tracy Kelliher's dad, if you must know. Tracy Kelliher's dad was so mad at me. I tried to tell him that nothing happened, that I'd decided that being dead and un-being were two different things and I didn't want to be dead, I just wanted to be less me and more *not* me, and I realized I didn't have to get hit by the bus, I could just go away on it. He didn't understand. He must have thought I took a pill. He should have known me better! I've never been able to swallow pills! I hate pills!

In the hospital, I explained to a very nice lady doctor what had happened and she seemed to understand about the bus, which was a relief. Then Mom had to come in. She had crying circles under her eyes, which are like tired circles, but redder. I felt terrible for her. I mean, first her son steals sodas and next thing she knows, her daughter is rushed to the hospital for napping. I cried when I tried to explain about un-being and North Dakota. I cried so hard that I nearly choked to death on my own spitty weeping. Crying like that is not healthy. There's just too much phlegm. Mom stroked my back and my hair and murmured about starting over. Starting over, starting over, starting over.

By the time we left, I realized that starting over was even better than un-being. It was the answer. The bus was just a simile (or a metaphor). Within three days, the house had a FOR SALE sign on the lawn. Mom and Robby packed everything into the car that we were going to bring to our new life. Mom wanted to leave everything. She said everything was bought with money that wasn't ours, so it wasn't ours to take. That may well have been true, but I wish we'd brought the Xbox. What was brought to Texas turned out to mostly be dishes and photo albums and clothes. Nothing else. I guess that I wanted to start over, too, just like Mom said, because I left everything. That stuff belonged to the old Kammie. I wanted to be new. Someone else. I left everything, a mini museum of me. The only thing I wanted was the water bed and I couldn't take that because it wouldn't fit in the car. I stuck scissors in it before we left. It took a few too many jabs to be really satisfying, but I was happy when it finally made a sad *glub-glub* noise and water seeped out onto the floor. The real estate lady was probably furious when she saw that. It made me feel terrible to think of her face, but I couldn't just leave the bed. I felt like by stabbing the bed, I was also un-being the person I used to be to make way for the new me, if that makes sense.

On the last day, when I went into my room, I almost grabbed Ratty Catty, but then I didn't. I made myself leave it. Dad gave me that cat. *Good-bye myself*, I said.

Then we drove to Texas. The drive was hot and long. I threw up into a shopping bag in the backseat, and Mom and Robby sat in the front. When I got bored, I counted telephone poles out loud in

French. Robby told me to stop, but I ignored him. It was like Robby thought he was Dad now, minus the stealing from sick kids.

"*Vingt*," I said. "*Vingt et un, vingt deux . . .*" Then I threw up again.

Robby said, "She's barfing again," and shook his head, sadly, looking slightly annoyed, much like Dad used to do. *Well*, I thought, *at least I finally I hate him as much as he hates me*. No one wants to be Dadded while they are barfing into a nondisposable Walgreens bag, let me tell you.

"Leave her alone," said Mom, but that wasn't any more helpful than what he said. No one really wants to be alone at a time like that either.

We left a lot of things behind, but not enough. It turns out that you can't get away from yourself. The museum of you is inside you. It isn't stuff. It isn't a heavy phone with a curly cord. We left the house, the lawn, the water bed, Tracy Kelliher and her dad who had seen too much. Mr. Thacker. The grave where Hayfield was buried, wherever that was. I don't even know. Mom said the vet took care of it. Maybe there is a pet graveyard in New Jersey. If so, I'd never seen it. I'd like to. Maybe one day, I'll ride my bike there.

But I can't ride my bike there because we also left behind my bike. It had my name on a license plate that Dad attached behind the seat. I hated that license plate because it made me feel 6 years old. My dad didn't understand that I was past that now. That license plate made me cringe inside, but I didn't tell him, because I never wanted to hurt his feelings. How dumb was I? His feelings deserved it, and worse. The bike had a blue basket. Sometimes I'd put Hayfield in the basket and ride around. He liked it. But now Hayfield is dead. Even if he were alive, I couldn't ride around because I cannot feel my feet and would not be able to pedal.

It's true. I can't even feel my feet anymore.

It's possible that the goats have chewed them off.

Suddenly, there's another voice, thundering above me like another god, "We have to stop digging! I think the well might collapse!" The scrape, crash, vibration of the earth had already turned into music for me, which I only noticed when it stopped.

Oh, I think. I close my eyes. I am sleepy, as sleepy as I felt after talking to Mr. Des on the help line. And if a well is going to collapse on you, it may as well happen while you are dreaming you are somewhere else, someplace happy with a lot of trees. North Dakota, maybe.

9

BE A GRAPE

I wake up and it's eerily silent, so right away I know that I'm dead. I'm dead in a pile of rubble. I'm crushed.

Except I'm not. I'm not dead. There is no rubble.

The well didn't collapse. The hole is lit from without. That's like the opposite of being lit from within. I don't know what it means. The light is pouring in and down, trickling into my eyes like tiny swords, stabbing. The samurais have moved up from my ribs then. I breathe. No, they are still there.

They must have called in for reinforcements. The entire Japanese army is stabbing me. Are samurais Japanese army guys or did I make that up? I don't know anything.

I blink and blink and blink and blink. I feel slow and thick and empty and light, like a heavy balloon with the air taken out, and where did everyone go?

"Lassie," I whisper. I miss Rory Devon (the cat, not the singer). Will I ever be lying on my bed in the orange room again, with The Devs pawing my face to wake me up? Cats are always hungry. That's the other thing about cats.

I don't want to be dead. I don't want to un-be. I don't even want to move to North Dakota. I wanted that before, but that was a long time ago. You'd think that in our fancy house with the water bed and the big TVs and the pattern-mowed lawn that I'd want to live, but the thing is that back then I didn't. Now, in the trailer life we have in this terrible dusty warehouse town, I do. It doesn't make sense. What does? Nothing. I don't want to be dead in a well. I don't want to be friends with Mandy and

Kandy and Sandy. I want to grow my hair out again and just be me.

Maybe I could learn to sing. Record Store Dave teaches guitar lessons. I could play guitar and sing with flowers in my hair, and maybe go to outdoor concerts and meet a boy to love forever. Mom and Dad met at a concert. They said there was a lot of mud and shouting. They said people hugged and lit fires and roasted marshmallows and did crazy things and regretted it. They said the tents sagged under the rainwater and you couldn't hear the music much anyway. But they fell in love, regardless. They fell in love, and then left and went to Denny's and ate Moons Over My Hammy. I guess it was sometime after that that Dad went bad. I wonder if Mom still loves him. I wonder if outdoor rock concert love is the kind that goes the distance, even after one of the people involved turns out to be the Devil himself, at least according to elderly women in the supermarket.

The silence is shivering over my skin. I've stopped shaking. I'm not even cold. The light is warm. It's the headlight on the train that's going to hit me. The deadlight. Or maybe it's the sun. Duh. It's the sun! It's tomorrow. It must be tomorrow because it has already been night. The sun is at the perfect angle to glow down the well and onto my head, burning the fleas who are currently layered up with SPF 50 and reading home decorating magazines and planning their next thigh-slimming diet.

Then there are voices. Thank goodness. I'm not alone. They won't let me die down here. They won't! I know it. Mr. Des will save me. Mom might not have time because she has to go to work. That warehouse doesn't give you sick days and I bet they don't give you days off when your kid is in a well. Poor Mom.

Robby won't save me because he's a jerk and I ruined his joke. And Mandy, Kandy, and Sandy won't! They'll get too much mileage out of a dead best friend club-member! Oh, I hate them. I am burning with hate.

"KAMMIE!" booms a voice. "GOOD MORNING! HOPE YOU ARE OK DOWN THERE!" It sounds like a morning-host on a radio show. Goooooooood morning, Nowheresville! I wonder if he'll spin some records. I wonder if he'll dance.

We listened to the radio in the car all the way to Texas. Mom said, "Enjoy it now because pretty soon we'll be taking the bus, and there's no music on buses." And then she nearly cried. "That is not a stiff upper lip," I said. She said, "You're not your dad, so don't act like him." But she stopped herself. And my insides curdled like cottage cheese.

"MY NAME IS COLONEL FRANK BAYLISS!" the voice booms. "I AM WITH THE NATIONAL GUARD AND WE ARE GOING TO GET YOU OUT OF THAT WELL!"

His words twinkle down on me like sparks from fireworks, with spits and sizzles. The National Guard! This is definitely going to be on the news. I feel a tiny surge inside, like that time I drank a Red Bull. I liked how it felt at first, like I was extra-awake, but after a while it just felt like jitters, and eventually it felt like I would not sleep for a week. I hate Red Bull. But his voice is like how Red Bull was for the first half hour.

I am going to live for sure now. The National Guard! "Do you hear that?" I say to the coyote on my head. "We'll be saved."

"*You* will," he says sadly. "I am not real."

"I can't wait to go home," I say. "I just want to see it. The wood paneling and the orange carpet with the worn-out parts and those cats all winding around my legs, their silky fur against my scratched skin, slinkily passing by."

"That's not a word," he says.

"Is so," I say.

"Say it in French, you traitor," he says.

"Le slink," I say. "If you love something, it becomes real. And I love you, *coyote d'argent*."

"*Je t'aime*," he says and sighs with relief.

Then I fall asleep again. But I keep waking up because I feel funny and my brain shakes me awake and says, *Drink from the tube of life*, and I say, *OK OK OK*. I sip from the tube. The more I sip, the more I feel like things are normal, as normal as they can be in a well. When I stop sipping, things swirl.

All the things: secrets and memories and spiders and zombie goats and whispers, forcing their way into my head from above.

The line between dreaming and waking up is all gone, erased, like an Etch-a-Sketch that your brother shakes clean right after you finally finish drawing a perfect picture. I hope a poor kid has that Etch-a-Sketch now. It also used to be Mom's. From her childhood. It was an antique! I hope that poor kid is drawing with it right now, and that it's not just locked up in a vault at the bank with my bubble bath and leaking bed. I hope all our stuff goes to cancer kids to play with. I hope right now our old pool is full of those dying, illuminated kids, laughing and splashing and glowing and floating around on inner tubes in the sun.

Voices tumble down on me. A voice dances up to me on a little cat's feet. It's Dad! Again!

Dad, I say in my head, *where did you go before?*

I had to go back for basketball, he says. *I'm getting really good. I scored 100 points.*

Is that true? I ask. *Because you're a liar, Dad. 100 points is a lot. That's 50 baskets.*

Everyone's a liar, he says, sadly, bleating like a goat. *Some of them were three-pointers.*

He smells bad, I'm not going to lie. Even compared to the goats. My lungs wheeze.

Dad, I say. *What happens next?*

Let's go home, he says. *The lawn is getting long.*

Dad, I say. *It isn't. I mean, someone else lives there now. We've been replaced.*

Everyone can be replaced, he says. *Even me. Your mom will meet someone.*

You're getting out eventually, I say.

I know, he says. *But it will be too late. That concert was a long time ago. I was a different person. Young. I had a beard. Your mom needs someone. Take her to the record store. Music helps.*

That's what I was thinking, I say. *That's what I wanted. I didn't want you to get forgotten, even though I would love to forget you because I hate you. Are all relationships this complicated?*

Yes, he says. *You know, you should hate yourself, too. YOU wanted to go to Disneyland. I made your wish come true. Doesn't that make me good?*

Dad, I say. *I didn't* mean *it. I didn't mean for some wishing kid to not get to ride on the teacups. I was just dreaming. It didn't have to happen.*

I messed up, he says. *I wanted to give you the world. I wanted you to love me.*

You stole *the world! I say. That was bad. I did love you. Now I don't know you.*

I love you, he says. *I wish I'd gotten you a pony.*

I love you, too, Dad, I say. *But you're a raisin. I'm glad you didn't get me a pony. I'm glad you didn't buy one. Don't lie about the basketball again.*

I know it, he says. *I'm a raisin. But in jail, I will fill up again. I promise to be a grape. I only scored 8 points.*

Be a grape, Dad, I say. *Be a grape. Practice your jump shot.*

You be a grape, too, he says. *You're a liar, too. You lied to get into that club. Everyone is a liar.*

I know it, I say. *I raisined. But just for a minute. Then I fell down a well. That's karma. That's what Tracy Kelliher would say.*

The Kellihers were nice people, he says.

Dad, I say. *They weren't.*

They were, he says. *We were just looking at them through raisin-colored glasses.*

I'm sleepy, I say.

Don't ever try to un-be again, he says.

I promise, I say.

I have a game, he says. *I have to go.*

Bye Dad, I say.

Bye sweetie pie angel, he says. *Stay grapey.*

Grapey, I say. *You too.*

Then the well collapses on my head. It starts off like a drizzle of rocks and gravel, but then it's a storm, sort of like the concrete sky is coming down to meet me, and I am standing still. It hits me, hard, a thousand ropes at once that aren't ropes, but actually rocks. It turns out the sky is heavy. In that split second before I black out, I know I am blacking out. I see silver, then light gray, then dark gray, then black. All the colors of the black rainbow, filling me up and covering me over.

I'm not dead, just so you know.

Just silver.

Like light. Like hope. Like someone leaving on the Number 7 bus.

10

InteRRupting ChicKen

This is what happened:

Where my right shoulder was pressed against the wall, the well suddenly gave way and I fell over sideways into a pool of light and dust and a man caught me cleanly. His name is Marty. It's not a very good name. Anyone would tell you that. I didn't know his name when he caught me. I didn't know I was awake. I thought I was dreaming. There were fish, nibbling, and then I was the fish. I pedaled so fast and hard on my bike that I got away, and I reached my hand into the deep freeze for another ice cream sandwich and Robby said, "Don't look up." And then the bats swarmed down and I was going to scream, but Hayfield jumped into my basket and I had to get away. Pedaling, falling, and then the wall and the light. I wasn't awake, but I wasn't not awake. Then there were arms. Marty's arms. My gills were useless in the air.

The dream and the thing that was happening in real life were the same, braiding themselves together in a fishtail, mermaid, French braid. Grandma was there, watching, eating cookies, her eyes twinkling with an almost-smile. (*Twinkling* is one of those details that I remembered later about Grandma. Maybe she had twinkling eyes in real life, maybe she didn't.) The dream swam with fish. I saw that the fish were beautiful. My lungs opened and closed, pulling for air through the dust and grime. Where was the air? I fell through the water bed, drowning, but I didn't want to un-be, not anymore. Please, no, not that.

Marty held on tight. Marty said my name, over and over again. Marty's arms were tree branches that bent low enough to pluck me up. "Baaa," said the zombie goats, clambering up to freedom. Goats are amazing climbers, you know. I think it's because they don't think. They just *do*. They're not like, "If I try to climb that, I could slip." They are already climbing. I knew I should *do*. Do what? I breathed in and in and in. I kept breathing until I was a balloon, red, floating high above the scene, which was packed with people and even TV camera crews from CNN filming my floppy, bleeding body in Marty's tree-trunk arms. *Well, isn't that nice. I'll be famous.* Mandy, Sandy, and Kandy were crying in a huddle, their braids newly tightened for the small screen.

It's hard to sort it all out.

An eagle swooped low with his beak open and I said, "Please, no!" but he still did it, he popped the balloon and *BAM*, I was back in my body, which hurt in so many ways, like I'd been folded too tight and, in the unfolding, I'd broken into a hundred pieces. My arms and legs just hung there. I felt like a praying mantis, bent and awkward, sticking out at odd angles, all over the place, giraffing, like Kandy. I told my arms to straighten up, but they didn't respond. "Come on," I told them. Still nothing. Fish don't have arms, so I guess it made sense.

Now, I'm on a stretcher and covered with a really hot blanket. It's too hot. Sweat covers me like my own personal ocean. That feels right though, now that I'm a fish. I miss Marty. Being held by someone is really something when you haven't been held for a while. Probably all fish feel that way. When Marty's hand touched my arm, my eyes opened wide and leaked all the hose water everywhere. He didn't mind. I guess he didn't. Who is he to mind? He's a hero. He'll probably get a medal.

Then Mom is here. "Mom!" I say, and she looks surprised to see me.

"Oh, Kammie," she says. She's crying. I've made her cry. She's started. What if she never stops?

"Don't cry," I say. "It's OK."

"OK," she says, and cries anyway.

Robby says, "Knock knock."

So I say, "Who's th—"

But before I can even finish, he yells, "INTER-RUPTING CHICKEN." I've forgotten how to laugh, which is too bad, because right away his face closes like orange curtains crookedly shutting and blocking out the light.

I rearrange my face in one way, then two, then three, until my face has all the expressions at once. "It's funny," I say.

"Thanks." He half nods, half glares. "Can we go now?" he says to Mom.

"No," she says. "We'll go with her."

So here we are, a family on the Number 7 bus going out of town, except the bus is an ambulance, taking us to the hospital. I miss Hayfield. The ambulance starts and I listen for it to bump into something, but it's hard to hear above the sound of the siren slicing through the air like knife blades, spinning. "Shhh," I say, but it doesn't hear me. I am lying down and Mom and Robby are on a bench, and no one says anything, and I tell the coyote to run before he gets run over. I whisper it loud in my head so that the silver thread of it can reach him like when you talk into a tin can tied to another tin can on a string. I hope he is safe.

There's so much air up here. Breathing is a relief, I can tell you that.

In the hospital, Robby fidgets with his watch strap and Mom rocks back and forth, like she is rocking me, but she isn't allowed to rock me because I have some broken parts. That's what the X-rays say. We all have broken parts, that's the truth, but mine really hurt. My arm and my leg and all my ribs on one side, say the X-rays. The X-ray machine is really beautiful. Not the machine itself, but the pictures on the screen. Up there, in the light, it looks like I am made up of pieces of glass that all band together to form the shapes of legs, arms, and ribs. There are little lines in almost everything. There's this song that Record Store Dave played me that says, "There are cracks in everything, that's how the light gets in." I guess that's also how it gets out. I guess that's also how I made my own stars down there in the well, leaking my silvery light all over the place.

After the X-rays, I get taken upstairs, then downstairs, then up, and then down. All the while flocks of doctors flap around me, their wings gentle against my face. That's nice. I like that part. The soft, being-taken-care-of parts. The medicine drips into my arm through a tube. I'm filled up with silver, it shines through all my veins and everywhere. It's such a relief.

The trouble is that time is opening and shutting like a black hole, speeding up and slowing down, stretching inside me like a cat yawning. I lose a day or two days and I wake up and go to sleep. Mom is there and then she isn't. Robby is and then isn't. The hands on the clock twirl around and stop.

"Robby," I whisper, wet wool dripping down my chin. I clear my throat and the frogs hop free. "Robby, can we climb a tree when I get better?"

He looks up. He's been playing a game on his phone. I don't know what it is. I want to ask, but the words are too hard to figure out. "The trees here are crap," he says.

Ribbit, ribbit, I agree, but not out loud. I nod instead. I still feel mixed up. Which way do the words go?

"Maybe we can find one." He shrugs. "I guess we can try."

"OK," I say. OK OK OK OK. Those OKs bounce around the hospital room like Ping-Pong balls. In the distance, I hear sirens. They sound nice, like the kind of wind that holds birds up and sends balloons on journeys. I imagine the ambulances whizzing down the main street, like mine did, the person inside watching the whole town pass by backward and upside down, like moving through time in reverse. Mr. Thacker told me once that time can go forward or backward, that somewhere there is a parallel universe where time goes the other way. It made sense when he said it. But when I think about it, it falls apart. How can time go backward? Can people get younger? Can they unfall into a well?

"We should get some records," I say to Mom, who is there beside me. Her hair is flattened on one side like she slept in a chair, which I guess she did. "And a record player."

"We'll get one in the new house," she says.

"New house?" I say.

"I found a place to rent," she says. "It has a yard."

"Can we have cats?" I say, my heart full up with fur and fear.

She half-smiles. "Yes," she says. "Cats."

"Good," I say, and then I'm sleeping again, curled up on the gold-flecked floor in the sun, cats pressed all over my body, like gentle living cushions, carrying me home.

I dream about Dad, mowing the lawn. He's wearing handcuffs. It's hard for him to push the mower, but I can't help him. I shout at him to stop, but he doesn't answer because he's wearing ear buds that are attached to this huge record player. On the label of the record, the word SILENCE spins in circles. Dad sweats and pushes the mower and the grass grows and grows.

The real true reason why we moved to Texas is because the prison is behind the warehouse. The prison is right here. This is how it is now. Mom goes to see Dad on Saturdays. Robby and I do not. We aren't ready. Maybe we will be one day. That day is not yet. The rest of the week, she packages up stuff, stuff, and more stuff into cardboard boxes in the warehouse. She comes home with cuts on her hands from the box cutters. She comes home with blisters splitting open on her feet like eggs. She comes home and puts food in the fridge and leaves for her other job where they call her Deena the Dancer. I think she likes herself best as Deena the Dancer. She hates beer, but she likes to have the job, and she dances while she works. I think maybe she shouldn't because she already has blisters, but Mom is Mom. I can't stop her. Mom's name is Deena. Dad used to call her Dancing Deena. She always liked dancing, but when he said it, he was trying to be funny. I think her coworkers now just call her that because she literally dances while she stirs. Dad wasn't literal. He was always making something mean something else.

Dad was always trying to be someone he was not. I do that, too. I *did* that. I was trying to be an _andy. I'm not an _andy. I'm Kammie. I like skating and horses and climbing trees and riding so fast on my bike that my hair ripples out behind me like the wake of a boat. I like dogs and cats, and I even like Rory Devon (the cat *and* the singer), even though it's not cool to admit it. I've lied. I've been a liar. I don't want to be a liar. I'm not my dad.

"I'm not a raisin, Mom," I say, in my dream, but I guess it leaks through because I open my eyes and her face is a walnut that cracks open with a smile and I add, "You're a nut."

And she says, "You are, too."

And together we say, "Let your freak flag fly." Her walnut face breaks open wider still and I see that inside, she's a chocolate chip.

"I hate raisins," she whispers and her voice is soft like cotton, like a rabbit. "I like my cookies with chocolate chips. We'll make some. When you're home."

"We will?" I say, but my ribs hurt each time I breathe in.

"I can take a day off," she says. "I'll take a day off and we'll make cookies and I'll take them to your dad. He's allowed to have cookies."

"We can keep them," I say. "We can eat the cookies."

"We can share," she says. "Just one."

"Just one," I say.

The siren sings outside. The medicine drips into my arm. Inside me, the silver melds my bones together, leaving shiny perfect scars. I sleep and wake up, and wake up and sleep, which is the first step to being better. To going home and cleaning out the oven. To mixing up that cookie batter, the raw egg spinning in the bowl until it foams, the flour turning it into dough, and us adding the chocolate chips, like we used to do, back when we were rich and didn't have anything we thought we had, back when we were raisins.

"I love you," she says, but I'm already asleep when I say, "*Je t'aime, Maman.*" I'm already dreaming. Sometimes, in dreams, the fish are the best part, the way the sun shines down through the water at them, the way they dart like they are flying, soaring into the waving weeds of silent sound that vibrates all around them, always, the music that plays below the surface of everything.

11

Me

While I am in the hospital, Mom and Robby move the cats and all our things from the trailer into the house, so when I get to go home, I go to a new home. The new house is yellow. The paint flakes on the outside like dandruff, drifting down onto the concrete walk that goes all the way around the outside in a square. There are four leggy rosebushes trying to climb up under the back window, which is the window to my bedroom. It's the best room because of the way the sun shines in through that window in the afternoon. When I walk into my room for the first time, those darn cats are all over my bed, like a pile of laundry, spread out everywhere. I breathe in the cat smell of them. The litter box is in the basement. The house has three floors: basement, main floor, and the attic upstairs, which has been converted into my mom's new bedroom. The walls are white and there are sheer curtains on the window that billow in the wind.

"Mom," I say. "This room." I don't know how to tell her how great it is. I don't know how to say thank you.

"You know," Mom says, "I always imagined this room. I just never imagined that it was in Texas." I laugh, even though it's not quite funny. The fact that she's trying to be funny is worth throwing a giggle her way.

For a few days, I get to stay home while she goes to the warehouse. She got a promotion there and quit the brewery. Now she's a warehouse supervisor, just like Kandy's dad. She says he doesn't say much to her. She says that sometimes he sweats so hard that his plaid shirt starts the day one color, like orange, and ends it another, like dark red.

"That's completely gross," I say.

"He's nice enough," she says.

"I bet he doesn't smell nice," I say, and she smiles wide enough that I can see the fillings in her back teeth.

There's a tree in the backyard, but Robby and I haven't climbed it yet. "I'm thinking about it," he says, when I ask. "Leave me alone." But he brings home broken pallets from behind the warehouse. He brings home tools and nails. Soon, I think, we'll start to build. Soon we'll have a place to stand, where we can look out into the neighbor's yards, where we can see things that will make us better. Maybe.

"When?" I say.

"God," he says. "Give me a break, OK, Kammie? Everything isn't about you." And he goes into his room and slams the door so hard that the silver linings on all my bones shiver like glitter inside me.

"When?" I say, following him, and I think I maybe hear him smile, just a little.

"I'll tell you later," he says, and disappears into some music that he's playing too loud through the speakers that Record Store Dave loaned him.

Then one day, Record Store Dave comes for dinner. I'm not sure how it happens or why, and I don't care. I think maybe my wish worked, in the well. I threw myself in, instead of a coin, so of course it did. I have to count for more than a dime.

Record Store Dave dances with me in the kitchen, his beard moving a bit while he sways. He has piercings in his ears and he wears black glasses. "Hipster," says my mom, but she's teasing. She *likes* him. Dreams come true, I think to myself. Sort of. Not all dreams are Disneyland. It's just dinner, it's not Happily Ever After, which might not exist. Grandma used to say, "Happy endings are for fairy tales." Everyone is wrong sometimes, even Grandma. Record Store Dave dances with Mom in the kitchen, too. That's a lot. That's something. Her smile is silver and it glitters in the candlelight.

Dad writes me an e-mail. *Thanks for the cookies. Your mom says you baked them*, it says. *I hear*

you fell down a well. Brave girl. Love, Dad. That
is it. I read it over and over again. I don't know
what it means. *I hear you fell down a well. Brave
girl.* Was I brave to fall or brave to get out? I didn't
have a choice anyway. I was just a passenger. I just
happened to take the ride.

On my first day back at school, I see Kandy at
the entrance. She's smiling and waving. At *me*. I
walk closer. "So that's how it's going to be," I whisper. "Thought so." I try to make my face smile, but
it won't do it. I try to remember what I meant to
do. I try to hate her. I don't have to try *that* hard.
When I get close enough, I can smell her Smash Hit
perfume. Her hair is braided tight around her face,
so tight it's pulling her eyebrows up, making her
look surprised.

Everyone is staring. I don't know *anyone*. I
never bothered with anyone but The Girls and now
I'm alone.

I pause in front of Kandy, still deciding.

Then her eyes go up to my hair. (Mom let me dye
the tips of it silver. "You look like a hedgehog," said

Robby. "No, she doesn't," said Mom. "She looks like a dream.")

I touch the ends of my hair and think about what I'll say next. *I hate you.* Or, *Hi.* I'm kind of torn. I'm kind of scared.

Then Kandy smirks. "Your hair," she says. "It's so super . . . *interesting.*"

My hair is soft, like a cat's fur. It's grown a bit in the last six weeks. Mom trimmed it carefully to hide the flaws. It isn't great, but it *is* pretty, in a weird way. In my way.

"Thanks," I say. "I like it."

Kandy makes a sound, like she's choking on something she's trying not to say. "You would," she says, letting the laugh out.

I keep walking. I don't look back.

I walk past Sandy and Mandy at the door to the main office where I go to pick up my new schedule. The semester has changed and the classes are different now. My legs feel funny, like I'm walking on the moon and I'm wearing the wrong boots. Gravity is either too much or not enough. I want to go home, but I can't. This can't possibly be scarier than the well. My heart is racing like goats trampling in a herd.

I miss you, my friend, I tell my imaginary coyote. He's gone, but it doesn't matter. I mean, I made him up in the first place, so he can always be here if I want him to be.

My first class is art. The door is heavy and when I finally swing it open, the room smells like pastels and wax. I walk in and everyone stops talking and stares. I don't know what to do with all those eyes, nibbling at me all at once, wanting something. I think about Mom. *Let your freak flag fly*, she'd say. *Weird is wonderful.*

"Hi," I say to the room. It comes out croaky, like I'm still in the well. *Ribbit, ribbit*, says the frog. I clear my throat and start over. "Hi. I'm Kammie. I'm the girl in the well. The girl in the well is *me*."

There is a silence and then slowly, a boy in the back starts clapping. Then someone else. Then another person. My eyes fill up with tears because I didn't expect anyone to be nice. Not really. Because they know about Dad. Of course, the news put *that* story together. The embezzling, the sick kids, me in the well. I thought these kids would hate me, like Tracy Kelliher. I thought they'd think I deserved it.

I meet the eyes of the boy who clapped first and he grins wide, and his smile is like a door opening to a room I want to go into, but I'm scared of doing it. The seat next to him is empty. I make myself walk over to it, even though my legs are noodles. Each step is totally impossible, but I do it somehow. I sit down. My ribs are throbbing. "It takes months for ribs to heal," said the doctor. "Just try to keep breathing normally." "Even when it hurts?" I said. "Even then," he said.

I breathe. I pick up a pastel that's lying there on a blank white piece of paper. I start to draw. The pastel is soft in my fingers, and smooth. I don't know what to draw. I make shapes.

"Hey, Well G-g-girl," the boy says. He has those glasses, like Record Store Dave, and a stutter that I like. He takes a deep breath. "I'm Axel. I'm new."

"Hi," I say. "I guess I'm sort of new, too?"

He nods.

I know that I'm blushing because he's cute and he's talking to me and I can't look right at him, it would be like looking at the sun. After I got out of the well, I saw tiny sunspots on everything for days. I still kind of get them, like shadows of a dream that's already slipping away, scars burned into my retinas that make little memory ghosts. I keep my eyes on the paper. I color over the pattern of dots that I see. I like the way the drawing flows out under the soft end of that pastel. I like the way the colors slide onto the white of the paper, filling it up. I like how it feels like something good is happening, finally, right there in the art room at Nowheresville Middle School with the hot Texas sun shining through the window, illuminating the dust from all of us, drifting up toward that dazzling light outside.

Acknowledgments

When I was working on this book, my daughter Lola (then seven) asked me what I was writing. I told her, and she said, "That doesn't sound very good, Mum. You should add a talking dog." So I added one, as well as some zombie goats and other creatures. Thanks, Birdy-girl.

One day I clicked on a story on my Facebook feed about Baby Jessica (who is now an adult), who fell down a well in Midland, Texas, in 1987, and I immediately remembered how powerful that news story was and how we talked about it on the playground and how the whole world was caught up in her rescue. And then I thought, "What if I wrote a book from the point of view of a girl who is stuck in a well?"

On my dining room wall, I painted this quote from Roald Dahl's book *The Minpins*: "Above all, watch with glittering eyes the whole world around you because the greatest secrets are always hidden in the most unlikely places. Those who don't believe in magic will never find it." I encourage everyone to never forget to use their own glittering eyes. Ideas are everywhere. They are sometimes fleeting, but sometimes they stay tangled with your own imagination, and then they come together and form stories. That is where magic lives: in the weaving together of something you remember and something you heard and something you dreamed and something you saw once on Facebook and a character who you can suddenly see with perfect clarity, who is waiting to tell her own tale.

Thanks to the brilliant and lovely Jennifer Laughran; to the astonishingly wonderful people at Algonquin Young Readers; to my readers; and most of all, to every librarian and bookseller in the world: You are all my favorites.